jack the modernist

Jack the modernist

by Robert Glück

HIGH
RISK
BOOKS

NEW YORK / LONDON

Library of Congress Catalog Card Number: 95-67406

A complete catalogue record for this book is available from the British Library on request

The right of Robert Glück to be identified as the author of this work has been asserted by him under the Copyright, Designs and Patents Act 1988

First published in 1985 by Gay Presses of New York

Copyright © 1985 by Robert Glück

This edition first published in 1995 by Serpent's Tail, 4 Blackstock Mews, London N4 and 180 Varick Street, 10th floor, New York, NY 10014

Typeset in 11pt Janson by CentraCet Limited, Cambridge
Printed in Finland by Werner Söderström Oy

for Phyllis

Excited

YOU'RE NOT A lover till you blab about it. From earliest memory I've been excited and lonely, like a membrane that needs a caress during love-making, one caress and then another. I met Jack at a forum in April, 1981; we exchanged eyes during the presentation while his arm draped around the back of the empty chair next to him as though it were a boyfriend. He cocked his head and a two day growth outlined a high delicate cheek; my life was bereft of that contour. During intermission my face lit up but he bounded past and wrapped a man in a bear hug that rocked them back and forth. Jack was short but he expanded, surrounding this man whose face, pinned against Jack's shoulder, suffused with pleasure and embarrassment. Jack's friend was suddenly famous. His struggle to disappear made him the center of attention; he didn't know what to do with his eyes and he tottered back a little when Jack released him.

I leaned against a door, thumbs hooked in my belt loops and forefingers starting two paths that converged in my crotch. I thought, 'Now I'm really alone.' The combined effect was supposed to register as passionate narrowed eyes clicking toward Jack on flamenco heels: Jack nodded and I parlayed tension into a few sentences about the forum. He replied, 'The Right correctly feels we threaten its unconscious life.'

I said, 'My flat's a few blocks away.'

Jack looked past me, smiling into the crowd. 'Let's read the *Divine Comedy* together out loud.'

'Jack, we hardly know each other—how about some TV and then sex?' We settled on a walk.

The next day he knocked at three-thirty but it was still spring weather. Yellow sunlight fell on his face; I touched the indentation above his lip, breathless. We took Lily, a big dreamy dog who lived the walk so keenly it became hers. I concentrated on Jack: Prep school and Harvard accounted for my pleasurable fear and his overalls and red chamois shirt; I knew others who used poverty for depth. In New York he worked in a famous theater troupe: 'We pissed on stage and took our clothes off.' My libido rushed forward to claim that information. I guessed forty by the skin on his hands. I talked brilliantly; he must be a good director, I thought, if he can enlarge people this way.

Lily checked resumes too—inhaled them from hubcaps and the corners of buildings, from strangers who stooped to admire her blond tail and ruff, her apricot ears. She scouted bones and delicious dabs of filth, slyly eyed children's ice cream cones, frankly implored construction workers in orange hats who sat on the sidewalk crosslegged behind their open lunchboxes; she searched their faces, trying to locate an invitation, eyes misting before the giant concept (fragrance) of chicken and ham.

'You'd be a fool to pass me up, Jack.'

Jack's features attempted a graceful bow off his face. He was small, slender, barrel chested, descended from French Jews. He looked like a sparrow, glossy black curls the color of raisins, bright black eyes and for a beak the small blade of a pocket knife, the likeness enhanced by a tendency to bounce on his toes. Or his face resembled a maraschino cherry, full of refined pep. I was so attracted I was bursting with news, personal news to launch intimacy—to put my hand where his body caught and softened the denim, for that to be a destination—so I recited my catalogue of ships: 'Two blacks, one Puerto Rican, two Irish Catholics (one of' them went on to S/M—he'd always said 'You can do whatever you want to me'—wasn't I already doing everything I wanted? Later he appeared with black eyes, etc.—he had great legs), one German Catholic, two WASPS (one was Episcopalian, the other from Los Angeles), one Japanese-German, one Marxist Art Historian, one

3

Chinese, one Italian and three little Jews. Jack, I always had a soft spot for little Jews with big noses, maybe because of my first lover; I loved Andy so intensely I used to wonder if I would be scarred. When he left the apartment I gathered up his cigarette butts and smoked them even though I didn't smoke. During puberty I kept hoping my nose would grow big. Everyone else in my neighborhood had a big nose.'

Jack's eyes *twinkled*. 'You can't depend on those biological clocks—don't stop trying, Bob—you may still get one.'

'Jack, I try. I answered a sex ad from the *Advocate*. The guy wrote 'For Love' and went on to describe himself as a small Jewish dancer. What could be nicer? When we met, he turned out to be a converted Jew. His nose was Portuguese from Salinas but he learned Hebrew and lived in Israel and he choreographed ballets based on Jewish legends like the Dybbuk. He had great turn-out during orgasm. I think we made each other nervous. I would say, 'There's a Jew in this bed!' And we wouldn't know if I meant a fallen Jew (me) or a believing Jew (him) or a real Jew (me) or a fake Jew (him). When he dumped me I wanted to sue for false advertising.'

I opened up in Jack a territory named Bob; I anticipated in me a sister city named Jack. He replied, 'I want a black lover—that's one reason I attended the forum.' He submitted this obstacle to our romance with the cheerful heartlessness of a folk tale. At once I was tired of my past and where it led me—a boring melancholy that trained me to be good at death. I'd exhausted my possibilities and nothing new started up; I could see why people kill themselves. My jurist's voice countered, It's not a *big* deal, and I had to agree: my writing's okay, friends, teaching. Writing, sex, money, friends—as we walked along I felt a vague guilt—I hadn't done justice to my experience. I wanted to trade on it, shabby currency. The way I told these stories exhausted me and I saw my lovers as a form of stasis. To make it more lifelike, I'd gladly have given a statue the past and the sarcasm.

A jay chided, aggressive. The aroma of wild fennel, a lure. A sportscar drove by, an impulse. Lily chased a cat, fun. We stepped off the curb. Our elbows touched, a hinge. Pieces of fog hung in a tree, perception. We walked across some grass—pastoral—and talked about the past—pastoral-historical. When we passed La Victoria the sky was parquetry of beaten gold. Our walk tired me out with its little steps; I wanted to take one giant step across town and into Jack.

'I'm sorry my list is so short, I was with Ed (Japanese-German) for eight years.' Identity seemed remote as the village our grandmothers came from. Ethnicity, storytelling—my lovers sounded like so many flavors, strawberry, lemon, lime . . . 'How about you Jack?'

'What about me?'

'Tell me where you've been, who you've seen, how they looked and what they said.'

'I had two lovers, one for six months, the other for a year.'

'Two?'

'That's it.'

'Two brief loves in a man of forty.'

'I'm thirty-four and I never met the right individual.'

'You seem to know everyone.'

If Jack described the other, I can't remember; something about a playwright or a producer, a nice guy. I only remember Joe-Toe. 'Joe-Toe is an actor who left a few months ago for New York, which to an actor equals breathing. What an actor means to New York is more like another sneeze for which someone may or may not bless you. I gave him the name Joe-Toe when I was teaching him to pronounce Giotto in a play I directed. He takes baths hot enough to make steam.' He rubbed (meditatively?) his two-day growth and his eyes relaxed on the distance. I figured they were still involved.

'Is he handsome?'

'Not really, he's funny looking.' Spoken with a lover's pride, I thought.

The buildings we passed were mostly nineteenth-century gingerbread and they understood each other in a cozy and irrelevant way that excluded their inhabitants and faltered before the existential glamor of a tract house or highrise. Jack lived in one of those bleak Victorian slag heaps around General Hospital, but the old staircase with redwood wainscoting remained and each landing had a lamp of hammered brass and stained glass. The first two were lit against the twilight but Jack's landing was dark. He hunted for his key, then knocked. Jack's roommate opened. Lily exploded into a blur of huffing and wagging and shot past him into the flat. She made a beeline down the hall and into a room where some finches cried out in alarm and bashed themselves again and again against the bars on the far side of their world, their voices piping a bright feeble terror. They had dark blue tails, red bills, baby blue sides and they gave off an odor of sage.

I caught Lily's neck and Jack held her rump—then he told the birds to sing for me, as though they were canaries! Lily's eyes rolled back in voluptuousness and she licked her chops with a moist pink tongue. We dragged her away, closed a door and outside that door she remained, titillated, absorbed, her downcast eyes conveying an impression of unseeing abstraction. Later, when I passed her on my way to the toilet, she turned away from my caress, unwilling to be distracted. Jack's roommate was a British law student studying for the Boards. He immediately vanished but his anxious smiles and incomplete gestures permeated the flat. Jack went into the kitchen to pour us wine. The kitchen was yellow—its cheerfulness more an academic point. The color said 'Life is Great' but was contradicted by shabby cupboards, weary linoleum, chipped dishes and cookbooks shelved too high for use. I explored his bedroom.

7

It was on the sunset side. Two windows spilled amber light onto four walls of books, a bed, a beige chenille bedspread, a small hill of brown corduroy pillows, a drafting table with a high stool and a file cabinet. The room smelled like chocolate, a sweet smell of books. I explored further: an analytical spirit asserted itself in the face of Jack's bed and the oblivion I intended to enjoy there. Self-preservation advised me to act fast, but there was nothing in the papers on his drafting table except for his handwriting. It was amazingly sleek and deliberate as set type: the y's descended and the r's ascended, flags and pennants. I could love that. I couldn't understand how he earned a living. From an envelope I learned his name was John. Jack was a nickname. I relished it: *Jack* is so flat, like a flat rock or a landing strip between the flights a sentence can make. I could love that. I was against his boots, they supplied a false amount of height to his small frame and made him bottom heavy. He had only overalls, the good pair and the bad pair. He covered his bulletin board with quotations and the heads of friends. His hair parted at the back. Soft clear voice. His eyes twinkled when he smiled because they scrunched up, gathering their liquid onto a smaller surface. Herbal toothpaste. A file cabinet. Small hands and feet. I figured that would stand me in good stead. I figured he would teach me and encourage me and smooth out my hysteria and distress. His library appealed to me as a source of great potential energy. The books stood two deep, shelved with a free hand—mighty classics and plenty of books I'd never heard of sped up my heart with their flirtatious glances. Then they lost their individual contents and became comprehension and speed. My throat tightened with a pang for the new life. I felt seasick. Many of the books I opened were signed by the authors and inscribed with a friendly note to Jack; in all of them Jack had circled passages. I love intelligence and eagerly fetishized Jack's; I half-reclined like a starlet. He returned with a glass in each hand and sang to the books, 'You made me love you, I didn't wanna do it, I didn't wanna do it.' He was addressing civilization.

'What do you trust?'

'Not who but what? Jack, I trust gossip.'

Jack sat next to me; he looked worried, said, 'Gossip is crude.' I reasoned that the depth he missed in a single story could be found collectively in a hundred. He cocked his head, attentive, so I became interesting. 'The people who know your story are as important as the plot. Gossip registers the difference between a story one person knows and everyone knows, between one person's story and everyone's. Or it's a mythology, gods and goddesses, a community and a future.'

Jack took my hand. That was exciting. I finally stopped smiling, let desire bewilder and reorganize us. He asked, 'What do you mean by community?'

'Ecstatic sexuality.'

'Whew.'

Sex was the reply to any question. Jack was problematic but great potential; he saw our relationship as the development of raw material. 'Let's do exercises together.' 'Let's study conversational French.' Svengali dives into Trilby's mouth, draws back astonished and cries, *Your palate is like the vault of a cathedral!* I wanted my soul thrilled— Jack was the man for the job. He talked freely and openly on every topic (but himself), displaying technique and an acquaintance not only with the world's knowledge but with its wisdom, which he circled. Jack swirled a purple crescent at the bottom of his glass, a sliver of wine slid down his throat, tannic. I wanted to follow. It would be a light comedy to pair myself again, the witty gravitational weights and balances of the twin star a couple makes. Still, I ached for Jack to engulf me and rewrite my life in bolder script. The tenderness I felt for him would chart out that impulse. There wasn't a single sentence that equaled the tenderness I intended Jack to bear me: only shared gestures over a period of time could express it.

I laid my tongue—my whole body—on his lower lip. We looked better without clothes. It was getting dark. We frenched for a while and then tipped backward onto the bed. I opened his hand and kissed his palm because my life seemed bereft of passion. Jack turned away—rightly I admitted. His hand slipped around my waist, a firmer pressure meant roll over, then it lightly skirted my ass. I didn't dare feel that much pleasure. I changed the subject by taking his cock in my mouth, leaning over him, absorbed as though he were a difficult book. I liked his cock, it had the clear smell of cut grass and it was refined as his other features so I could take it in easily. Each time I drew my tongue along the shaft a discreet spasm crossed his face; suddenly he sat up and broke into pieces, faced all directions at once; I thought Jack was starting to cry. It filled me with wonder. His face dangled midair, features rotating separately like the parts of a mobile, then he literally pulled himself together, nose, ears, two eyes, mouth. He stretched out on top of me and whispered, 'Put your hand on my lower back, lower, that's it, now the other on the back of my lungs.' I rose to any of Jack's occasions—I started to kid but he turned his head away and didn't speak; he initiated a long silence whose mournfulness I shared but couldn't interpret. I could have said, I love you. Jack's weight was like agreement. Beneath my hands his breath became sharp and fast.

11

Although I like to pitch and catch, I just wanted Jack *in* me. Accepting my body and the world took that form. His cock kept alternating between stiff and flaccid, a weathervane constantly shifting as we framed and reframed our attraction. We eroticized a finely-honed attention which challenged terms as soon as our bodies invented them, which addressed my sudden shifts of context, his mid-gesture costume changes. Instead of an oceanic welling with its always-in-the-future-until-it's-in-the-past crescendo, we remained moment by moment; we aroused Choice, crowned Wit—a woman can curtsey, a man can remove the hat from his head with a grand gesture while bowing elaborately—Wit, Choice and the Particulars. Our attraction for each other expressed itself as a problem to be solved, a topiary maze, each new distinction a turn in the inquiry until the pleasure grew so intense I had to look away. I would call that first lovemaking *dusky*, we kept slipping through each other's hands—hide and seek by moonlight—it was charming.

It charmed me; we ate, talked, showered, slept, more talk, more sleep, tomorrow, four or five nights a week, and for the first time since puberty my body was at rest. Jack simply converted without resistance or even a mood swing. When he called me up I felt like a contest winner. 'It's Jack. Want to go to dinner, a gallery, demo, movie, party, concert, café?'—whose worth we did or didn't agree on but with the same understanding and pitch; or Jack said 'great' and I said 'stupid' but to Denise and Bruce I found myself saying, 'a masterpiece.' I could grapple and I could surrender—that meant a lot to me. I pictured me at my full height and I intrigued and even aroused myself; teary and improvisational, I looked for developments that equaled my mood and waited to see what I would do next.

This concludes the first chapter of a love affair told with infinite safety from my house to yours, first person. From that beginning an image of Jack

12

remains that continues to define tenderness for me. Two cups and two plates, blue and white, disappear along with the pine table and the kitchen and the hall and the living room when I turn off lights one by one as though I were dispensing with every part of my life except Jack, lit by the 60-watt next to my bed. Jack, already a legend, lies on his back, sheet up to his waist, hands clasped behind his head, nipples—whole notes—floating above his rib cage, a vertical line of black curls insisting on symmetry, arms with their perfect flex, arms making delicate wings. He's hot— he's calmly waiting to have sex: I climb up beside him, pull back the sheet and run my hand along his hip. Suddenly everything shifts, his thigh moves with my hand, his buttocks shift down and toward me voluptuously and at the same time he sighs as his hip tips sideways like an Indian god, his balls slip over each other and his cock slides across dark curls. I feel very grateful. His breath is stepped up, lips parted and already a bit swollen, chest expanded, skin smoothed out, nipples whirling like gyroscopes—I want to cup them in my hand—whatever I do they will continue in suspension and motion—lips, skin and nipples taking on their sexual meaning, his dark eyes lively, interested, interpretive.

13

Breakfast: oranges, coffee and muffins
heating up. Bob opens the oven: are you
warm yet?

14   BOB: I DREAMT I was on a game show
that gave away sex prizes—the host from *Truth or
Consequences* spun a wheel trimmed with blue neon.
Shouts and applause. I was an average American,
naked, lying in a sling with my legs raised and my feet
in stirrups. The stage was an expanse of horizonless
beige linoleum with blue drapes at the wings. A truffle
imported from the South of France was inserted into
my asshole—a drum roll, scuffing and snorting in the
wings—and then—also imported from the South of
France—a pig trained to root for truffles—
JACK: Was the host Ralph Edwards, Jack Bailey or
Bob Barker?
BOB: You're a deep scholar. Is everything good?
JACK: Everything is perfect. Hi Lily.
(Jack puts a bit of muffin in his mouth, then imitates

her, expectant face, worried face, his head cocked, wagging its tail. Lily focuses; her nose works. He laughs and points. I ask *What's funny?* He says *Lily's at attention—Hi Lily.* She does not react except to the muffin's changing location. He holds the last piece inside his mouth for a long moment, then tosses it to her. She bites it out of the air. He shows her his empty hands saying *It's the international sign for no more muffins* and she turns away.)

BOB: No, everything *would* be perfect, Jack, if you just got down on your hands and knees under the table and gave me a blow job.

(Jack sends his eyes skyward and sinks beneath the pine in the measure of one exhaled breath. He finds me unbuttoned and soon I'm receiving messages from below the horizon. But Jack only licks it once or twice, then clambers back onto his chair. His eyes twinkle; it's a game. Jack had only two brief affairs and didn't trick, no baths, no bars. I want him to suck for a long time, for hours, until he becomes completely identified with it—like a starfish whose grip on the rock makes up the better part of its being. *I finally pry his face from my cock—his eyes dilated, expression subnormal, churning with desire and regret.*)

BOB: Artichokes, like figs, are not fruit, but flowers.

JACK (recognizes a gesture toward nothingness where distinctions are a joke. He makes fussy nesting and laying noises, viewing me from one eye, then the other, bird distinctions): The intellect delights in boundaries, Bob.

BOB (finds his civility irritating): I'm a wolf a snake a bat a horse: greedy, corrupt, with intense physical beauty.

(I want to pitch the energy so high something has to happen. I'm tired of being interesting, don't care if sex is pleasurable as long as it takes me somewhere new—)

JACK: To me you are this and more—

(Somewhere new—an excess in which my body goes rigid, eyes flicker like a home movie, time separates into frames, sounds sputter, a soft commotion like shuffling cards or a tumult of batting wings. I'm pleased to be told later that in fact I did ascend: 'Congratulations, from excess your body rose straight up seventy-five feet or more.' *I'm already on my way—I just don't want to be detained.*)

(We leap on the bed. I wrestle myself into a sitting position on Jack's big chest, rotate my hips and make goo-goo eyes and kissing motions, simian affection, but he merely sits up and I tumble backward. Jack says *Now I'm going to give you a garage.* He opens my jeans and puts my cock in his mouth and lets it sit there. My cock expands and my heartbeat claims a lion's share of identity. Finally he looks up and says *It's when you just park it. Is that a real thing?* I ask in a voice that's too close. He laughs at me and I reply *Just don't scratch the paint job, Bub.* He misunderstands— abandons the cock—but his hand falls *next* to it, immobilizing me. We're on our backs, out of breath, all my blood is far away and shallow from excitement. Finally Jack marshals energy for the next round.)

JACK (hoists himself on an elbow; with the expression of one who knocked on the wrong door): Excuse me, Sir, is this a great Romance silhouetted by the backdrop of History?

BOB: How was last night?

JACK (draws back from a kiss with a worried smile. As though to redeem an ordinary question with an extraordinary answer): I liked how your forearm touched my balls when you put your finger in my anus.

BOB: And?

JACK: And when you pressed against my prostate I thought I was going to piss but I know that's seminal fluid and I started dripping which I hardly ever do.

BOB: Jack, I have something serious to tell you.

(Jack's eyes leave the here and now; his smile disintegrates and the bottom half of his face chunks off its glacier and swirls downstream. I had great sex with plenty of people and liked them until our first serious conversation dismantled our future. Will Jack and I *have* a serious conversation?)

BOB: Jack, remember the Café Babar? When you said hello to your friends? They told you about their lives and then asked you what you've been doing. Instead of answering, you mentioned bumping into some mutual friend on the street in New York and filled them in on *his* life.

JACK: I didn't notice.

BOB: We've never had a personal conversation.

JACK: About what?

BOB: I don't know—ordinary things.

JACK: Such as.

BOB: Well, are your parents alive?

JACK: My parents?

BOB: What do they do?

JACK: My father was a lawyer; he died.

BOB: Of?

JACK: Cancer.

BOB: And your mom?

JACK: She's in New York.

BOB: Are you close?

JACK: I like her.

BOB: Does she have money?

JACK: Not much.

BOB: Sisters? Brothers?

JACK: A sister.

BOB: Older? Younger?

JACK: Younger.

BOB: Do you get along?

JACK: She's nice.

(How can Jack and I be so united in play yet share no other base? Our conversations are packed with subject matter but devoid of future. A future: will I know Jack's age then?—will he arrive for dinner on time? Will we relinquish the pleasures of cultural nuance for less upholstered sexuality where boundaries are really in question and the self returns refreshed? In the vacuum made by Jack's lack of story I project a likeness and tangle my heartstrings around it. Jack and I are continuous; we start out from a single cell, baked in the same pie, so I experience real difference as a betrayal, it always bowls me over. Or I project *difference* and love it. I'm sick to death of slow motion. I want speed—better, a trust fund, Fortuny gowns, summer homes. I enter on his arm, hello everyone! I never consider that Jack might not love me, so in response to his evasions I invent an increasingly complex Jack, a psychological Jack of telling detail. Same universe—different maps. One night I'm reading on his chenille bedspread when it suddenly dawns on me that all Jack's books are inscribed in his own ornate hand. I pull down *Moby Dick*; on its title page I read, 'For Jack and our friendship—Herman Melville.' I'm terribly confused and need an outside opinion.)

19

BRUCE: He seems a bit hysterical.

KATHY: He's *gorgeous*—I wish he was straight!

DENISE: He's smart. Nice eyes.

TOM: Bobby, he's a gorilla.

That afternoon Phyllis called

I IMMEDIATELY RECOGNIZED her voice.

At sixty-five Phyllis is enviably footloose. She has intellectual mobility, enough money, a house in Kensington, plenty of stamina. In fact, she has everything going for her—butterscotch voice and coloring, miles of bone structure, talent, children, the elbow room divorce provides. She called to say she wouldn't attend the next writer's workshop. Phyllis always sails off on obscure charter flights that are too good to resist or, more often, camps out in Lake County in Northern California where she grew up. I like to think her resilience comes from that landscape of small rugged hills and pear orchards. Once she sent a card from there: I'm in Lake County where even man is not vile. The present administration may not

be able to wreck this country, or find it. Affection-
ately—

'You're going to miss the workshop?—I
hope it's for fun.'

Her voice wavered. 'My son has been shot.'

'Shot?'

'He's been shot and killed.'

I didn't ask for details. I didn't feel I had the
right and didn't want to intrude. Self-consciousness
threatened to carve my response in stone. I said, 'I'm
so sorry.'

She answered 'I know' and we hung up.

I couldn't scramble down on the rug fast
enough. I was at odds with my body—practically
shouldered myself out of the way. I curled up and
cried. My crying was convulsed. I felt sunk. After a
while I unclenched; I remembered there was no one
home and wondered who all these tears were for. My
question wasn't so much a question as a symptom of
an ironic emotional structure with its cruelty of
design. The problem to consider was not whether I
shed tears under false circumstances but that there
were so many tears, they were so abundant and close
at hand. I cried hard, my face distorted and hot as
though I lifted a heavy weight, and I made hoisting
and heaving noises. Then for a while I cried ineptly,
mannered, noticing the thick world from my almost
subterranean perspective—my right eye level with a
surprising amount of gray dust on the dark wood of
the rocking chair rocker, dust which rocked back and

21

forth when the chair was rocking, I supposed. My left eye was level with an inch of blue velour thread that had caught in the nap of the red carpet. 'So that's where this blue thread is'—as though I'd ever wanted it, a flabby exhausted thought, as though I cared about a thread's flight through a vacuum cleaner. My mind wandered, unwinding thread, no light at the end of that tunnel.

I dozed off, then woke with a pang of loneliness so mastering I could only wonder. The center of my body was cooling, some internal heating system had failed, a chill right through my chest, stomach and groin. I lay on my side staring, my eyes fixed and stony from crying. I wanted to roll over but leave half my body where it was. The loneliness was so absolute and unexpected that I couldn't help wondering whose life this feeling belonged to. I kept shrugging as though I were telling the one responsible, 'It doesn't have anything to do with me.' I thought of Phyllis. But this was more like extreme age, no friends, no family, regret, approaching death. I wondered if I felt the extent of the pain whatever its source; probably just a fraction. I was ashamed of his death. I didn't know which of her sons had died and I forgot his name. I almost couldn't mention the death to anyone; instead I smiled and said something inappropriate, trying to deflect attention from it.

The Writing Workshop

I WALKED THE few blocks to my one o'clock Saturday writing workshop; a ghost town wind banged a shutter somewhere and pushed a balled-up newspaper down the middle of Church Street. The newspaper had a determined appearance but its stories were beyond repair. I couldn't tell these people what happened to Phyllis, it was beyond me.

The workshop consisted of about ten people on card chairs in a small Victorian room with hippie decor and the leftover odor of white jasmine or bayberry or lavender incense. I liked the camaraderie; we used that recognition to fuel our writing and to go further. But I wondered where we were headed: Will life be better when I *trade* on my image?—a self blurred by the isolation of naming. There's Rimbaud's 'I am really from beyond the grave' and Charles

Manson's 'You can't kill me, I'm already dead.' Their risks made the irreversible happen, then they offered us their enormous selves—in the spirit of revenge. Was death shorthand for an absolute that lacks a name? The giant feeling of being against society, language, self, became an allegiance with death. (Can this be true?—The world, refused, gathers there.) If this death is a murder, should the felony go on the record of the one speaking or the one addressed?

To demonstrate literature's splendor and propose as many ways of writing as I'm able, I begin the workshop by reading a passage or poem by a writer who interests me. I try to make it eclectic— Raymond Chandler, Judy Grahn, Peter Handke, Chaucer, Kathy Acker, Diderot, Wordsworth, Zora Neale Hurston. Writing channels the world into words once it's understood how piecemeal we are, like gossip, bits and fragments from beyond the grave, added, circulated, altered and withdrawn for the sake of expediency or in the spirit of revenge or in response to an absolute that lacks a name. Embracing that thought is embracing the world. That Saturday I brought the *Mabinogion*.

Pwyll waited on the mound. Soon they could see a lady on a big fine pale white horse, with a garment of shining gold brocaded silk upon her, coming along the highway. Her horse had a slow even pace. 'Let one of you go and meet her,' said Pwyll, 'to find out who she is.' One of them climbed down to the road and followed her on foot but the faster he ran the farther away she was. He returned to Pwyll and said, 'Lord, it is idle for anyone in the world to follow her on foot.' 'Aye,' said Pwyll, 'go to the court and take the fleetest horse thou knowest and go after her.'

Off he went. He rode out to the level plain and showed his horse his spurs. The faster he went, the farther away she was, yet she maintained the same pace that she started with. His horse flagged, he returned to Pwyll. 'Lord,' said he, 'it is idle for anyone to follow yonder lady. I knew of no horse in the kingdom fleeter than that, but it was idle for me to follow her.' 'Aye,' answered Pwyll, 'there is some magic meaning here. Let me go towards the court.'

They repeat this the following day. On the third day: Soon they could see the rider coming by the same road, in the same guise, at the same pace. 'Ha, lad,' said Pwyll, 'I see the rider. Give me my horse.' He assumed that at the second or third bound he would overtake her. He drove his horse to its utmost speed, but the faster he went, the farther away from him she was.

Then Pwyll spoke. 'Maiden,' said he, 'for his sake whom thou lovest best, stay for me.' 'I will, gladly,' said she, 'and it had been better for the horse hadst thou asked me this long since.'

The workshop sat forward, familiar gestures passed between them as if they lived the same life. The story seemed plucked from the center of a dream. It's not with strength or valor or magic or enchantment that Pwyll detains his ladylove; all his straining

forward does not equal a small gesture of communication, although it gives that gesture a wonderful
import. In the meshing of right gesture to right
response, meaning has been drawn back, tensed like
an arrow in the bow—arrows, eros—the string is
released and communication sails forth, a beautiful
ineffable happiness. Desire equals meaning in a
cruder, simpler way than we might be comfortable
believing (Cupid, draw back your bow).

When Jack showed me this passage he also
sat alert, as if the next step in the dream logic were
my response. He cocked his head and his high
expression had the finish of sculpture. I felt a tender
explosion of meaning. I kissed Jack seriously and
aroused him with my hands and lips. Pleasure is close
to awe, I bowed my head. He 'let me' take his cock. I
said, 'Whew Jack, this meat is so heavy I can hardly
lift it.' (Jack's cock: on which so many emotions hung
their hats. When I describe my feelings I look up and
extrapolate backwards from my current boyfriend's
plotline with its own twist and moral taste and future.
Jack flattens in the memory, loses his time and breadth
along with my attendant emotions, like clothes put
away, two dimensional on hangers in a closet.) In my
mouth it stirred, jumping to the soft drum of his
heart. I loved to suck his cock: the sheer exhilaration I
feel each time of finding and *having* what pertains to
me, what I pertain to. Its authority is so commanding
it can afford enticement and subtlety. I want to tell
you who I am; I want to be told who I am: the rock

bottom agreement that rejects any possibility of substitution whether it is a cock or a lady's shoe or a lover or a baby or a statue of the Virgin—to refuse all meaning in favor of this meaning.

The world, refused, gathers there, generating endless fertility of metaphor which supports rather than challenges the inevitability of Jack. I grab his cock, unpromising, and he says in mock bewilderment, 'What's that?' As it hardens I answer for him, 'It's my appendicitis, my inchworm, my slug, my yardstick, my viola da gamba, my World Trade Center, my banana, my statutory rape, my late string quartet, my garden god, my minaret, my magnum opus, my datebook, my hornet, my Giacometti, my *West Side Story*, my lance, my cannon, my nose-job, my hot dog, my little sparrow, my worm on the sidewalk after a storm, my candle, my Bic, my unicorn, my drawbridge, my white whale, my tuning fork, my divining rod, my cobra, my tooth, my noun, my horn, my asparagus, my vertical, my cyclops, my podium, my Picasso, my torpedo, my necktie, my subway strap, my intravenous injection, my lead singer, my church steeple, my bread stick, my chew stick, my joy stick, my beak, my shark, my trick guest chair, my metronome, my spout, my obelisk, my credit card, my sugar cane, my candy cane, my battering ram, my Roto-Rooter, my cigarette, my weasel, my fatherless child, my National Guard, my Rodin's *Balzac*, my fillet of gold, my meat thermometer, my submarine, my licorice stick, my fetish,

27

my tree, my tuber, my piccolo, my flag pole, my bean stalk, my pipecleaner, my Spruce Goose, my Mother Goose, my *Venus of Willendorf*, my sandman, my whip, my hatrack, my electric eel, my boy scout by the campfire, my genie, my compass, my stamen, my newel post, my date palm, my Dark Tower.

I stopped a moment and looked at it—an elegance completely trustful of itself, erect and shiny. It equaled the intensity I was able to feel. I don't have a language to describe that intensity so I lack the thought. No wonder Jack, familiar out of bed, seemed like a stranger. What did I want from this flesh peninsula that made me so urgent? Sucking, stroking—a hopelessly inadequate language. I felt like biting it and shaking it by the shoulders and lifting it by the waist. I wanted to be its executioner and mourner. The concept of pleasure didn't touch the engagement and physical call: to touch it like the neck of the *Winged Victory*—a shower of blue sparks; to use it as a face cloth, a scrub brush; to bank it like money. I wanted it to be a place: to be unconscious there, to sleep there.

It held a certain nostalgia for me like all the places where I picture myself asleep—like adolescence when I burned for abstract cock, the deity of arousal. Now I think I mean union beyond Jack so absolute it lacks a name. Pleasure carried him toward me. I turned and fled into my body—by that I mean I 'gave him' my ass. He followed, looking gloomy and severe. I fled, he followed: I squatted and his arm circled my waist, controlling my body, his cock deep in my ass, in my very center. To see us you would think piston and valve, except there's flesh on the inside and flesh all around so that's something different. The more you get fucked, the more you want it; eventually the pornographic *hungry hole* becomes merely accurate. I was surrounded by an O sound that was at once the voice of sex and the shape of the orifice he pounded. I saw myself as a bobbin winding and unwinding yet my orgasm was removed and extraordinary: I am visiting a country that always exists beyond me. I approach it with increasing familiarity because I have been in exile and this is my primitive home; in fact, its familiarity comes to equal myself. I decide I want to settle down forever. What can you say about a permanent resi- **29** dent? First, he breaks the social contract; second, we all are mainly interested in our own pleasure. Our lovemaking was not so much an achievement of communication or affection as of imagination. Jack and I certainly inherited the riders and the huffing and puffing and enchantment—the bric-à-brac of romance.

The passage from the *Mabinogion* threw into relief most of the workshop writing. I didn't have the words to tell them about the death of Phyllis's son; they shared my depression but not my lack of articulation: 'When I sleep my legs and arms go numb.' 'Any emotion is a prison.' 'I hit my fist against the wall but I feel no pain.' 'People move away from me, suspicious.' No one was ashamed to be brutal or indistinguishable; a coherent life seemed inappropriate yet no refinement of individual misery lacked words which, it was assumed, would also describe the world. The expression of pain is a sign of life. These adventures in psychic distress were as enchanting to me as Sinbad's voyages or the tales of Pwyll. I made their fragments into a pillow to lay my head on. But soon we became excited and jaunty inside this carnival of negativity—exhilaration of understanding outstripped the content of that understanding—an appetite for chaos—Pwyll and the maiden and the big fine horse and all our metaphors got vaporized by a blast of whiteness that parodied the penetrating light of spiritual illumination. It makes my head spin—a wind will eventually carry us away—

30   But Mildred, Jeanne and Peggy felt sad when someone wrote about distress. They were older, they wrote about the past or rural or ethnic lives and their characters mattered in a way that I could appreciate from afar. They mattered in a way that enabled narration from the middle distance rather than the ellipsis and grueling close-up of 'modern' literature, the thrills and spills of perception. Is time circular? Is it an explosion? When I write about Phyllis I also narrate from midway, it's hard for me to do otherwise. She demands a realism complete with revelation by character and epiphany that would not suit Jack. Still, this realism perceives with an unreal acuteness and consistency. How do I mesh modernism's disjunction with continuity and depth of feeling? I'd have to add a sub-plot which duplicates the first explosion that began story and time: the body. I feel especially close to Phyllis and take as health her instinctive love of community life, at however many removes. I feel an urgency to know personalities that include the passage of time. I borrow their sense of the future which makes storytelling possible. And wasn't it through Phyllis that I first cried for Jack?

'Uh, perhaps this poem would be stronger if the line about blisters and hair loss were above the one in which you're blown into the air?'

'Where's the fireball—a fireball pushes the wind.'

'Well,' someone laughed, 'being projected is way better than getting vaporized. Save vaporized for last.'

'Being projected? That's seven miles.'

'Where do you become water vapor?'

'Vaporized—no that's just fourteen miles.'

'*Blind* is fourteen.'

'Being projected is fourteen.' We were becoming giddy. The discussion took on the uncontrolled quality of laughing at a laugh.

'Seven, it's seven. Seven is vaporized, the next seven your clothes burn off and you go blind.'

'No no, first you're a missile projected two hundred yards—'

'Two hundred yards and *then* your clothes burn off.'

'Two hundred yards or two hundred miles per hour?'

Rainbows surrounded us. A crystal that hung by a string in the bay window—part of the room's new age paraphernalia—caught all the sun and released it in hundreds of slowly revolving arcs. Their colors were extremely pure and pleasurable, color carried by light instead of pigment, violet inside and red outside. The rainbows were so orchestrated—had so much presence—that their silence surprised and silenced us. They gave us access to the sorrowful import of our disorder and took the heart out of our dance of death. But we had duly absorbed the horror; it became part of our bodies like the shock of a slammed door or the tearing screech of brakes, two seconds of silence, a crash that doesn't happen: a voice says *file that*.

I walked home and sat down on my bed. My troubles were too numerous to consider all at once, their sheer quantity defeated me. My mom would say, 'Write a list, get a handle on your problems, deprive them of their active ingredient, time.' So I found a clean page in my yellow legal table and also the No. 2 pencil I swiped from Jack because his teeth had marked the wood. They were Jack's teeth but anyone could have done as much; I stole that intimacy and generality as a talisman. Nuclear catastrophe, destitution, famine, additives, melanomas, losing face, U.S. involvement in El Salvador and Nicaragua, Puerto Rico, South Korea, Chile, Lebanon and Argentina, war in the Middle East, genocide of Guatemalan Indians and extermination of the native peoples of Brazil,

I relinquished the firm barrier that separated us – no, that separated me
from nothing (p. 55).

C. Allen Gilbert's *Vanity*.

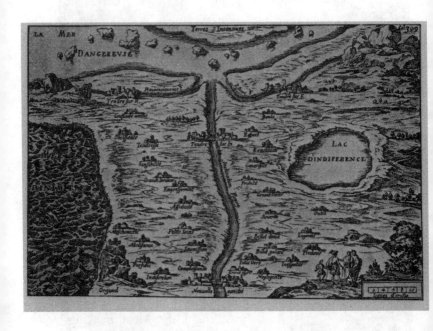

My map includes Jack's apartment, Leadville, Colorado, and the Mouses' River and Farm (p. 66).

Carte de Tendre, from Mlle. De Scudery's *Clélie*.

Philippines, Australia, answering the telephone, resurgence of the Nazis, the KKK, auctioning off the U.S. wilderness, toxic waste, snipers, wrinkles, cult murderers, my car, Jack's safety, queer bashers, South Africa, being unloved, considered second rate, considered stupid, collapse of our cities, acid rain, the deforestation of the Amazon basin, nerve gas, the death of my mother, Poland, unsafe drugs, the CIA, herpes, PCBs, industrial hazards, oil slicks, killing of porpoises and sea life generally, baldness, the New Right, organized crime, lynchings, pogroms and rapes, the defense budget of the U.S.A. and the U.S.S.R., Phyllis, video war games, destruction of the atmosphere, wasting of the soil through agri-business and strip mining, my death, storage of nuclear waste, heart attack, snipers, intestinal parasites, my parents' financial worries, *my* financial worries, blue whales, California condors, Bengal tigers, the Left, my aging, the brutality of the U.S. Meat packing industry (if there's such a thing as Karma we've had it), speaking in front of a room, cancer, Jack's reticence, pollution of the Mediterranean, anal warts, raising my hand and asking a question.

Feel better? I lie back on my bed and let my breath out. There is not so much sensation as you might think, a subtle emphasis marks the borders of my body—hands, feet, crotch and asshole more emphatic, more receptors, more expectation. I try to picture my dead self hosting the irrepressible life of worms and maggots but my own life returns as a

33

shadow that only makes me more aware of feelings in inner mouth and tongue, my face pushing out, itchy skin above ribs, nipples like two pots gently stirred. Small pains and irritations begin to assert themselves, dull eyestrain and a throbbing above my right eye, itchy scalp. My right ball aches a bit. Lips and toes slightly prickly as if asleep. Soles of feet tingle and I hear/feel intestinal sounds like people moving around a house avoiding each other. I sort out the fretful noises—bird, heater, parents, electrical—before dismissing each as having nothing to do with me. I also feel/hear my pulse, my heart through my body as it continuously gulps mouthfuls of blood like a pious cannibal. Finally the high woodwind of empty room air arches between my ears. I wear hearing on the sides of my head. Does air have anything to do with me? Inhale. My first breath has the heavy lift of an airplane taking off. I try to locate some joy there but instead it is sluggish and unwilling—my breath does not satisfy me. Could that be true? I find that if I contract my neck muscles I can follow a stream of breath past my face and throat into my lungs where it releases a sparkle of pleasure. Can that be true? The pleasure is akin to the tension of being drunk, the body reaching toward further intoxication, but the feeling is localized and after all, pretty faint. Still, there would be an accumulation. I let out my breath again and the pleasure remains, a tension in the form of a deep hum that takes place at the same level as my breathing only next to it.

My friend Bruce gave a housewarming party

I WAS CORDIALLY invited, Sunday
afternoon from four to eight. Bruce had lived on Noe
Street about a year; the apartment was spacious, had
light, was a bargain. At last he sensed the possibility
of duration: he unpacked books and threw out the
cartons, bought furniture, put down rugs and gathered his friends. This was going to be a party and
Bruce intended to do it justice. A thoroughness that
usually tackled *Working Class Literature in the Thirties*
or *French Structuralism and the Left* addressed *House-
warming Party* and as usual Bruce produced a satisfy-
ing formulation. We had clam dip and crudités and
potato chips and napkins and fruit and that venerable
classic, homage to onion soup mix and sour cream:
California Dip. Shovel some on a chip and you have
sweet, sour, smooth, opaque, salty and crunchy in

unison. We had chairs and lighting. We had music to lubricate the conversation and alcohol to do the same. I was surprised by the number of people I didn't know, having known Bruce for a decade, but I remembered that he likes to visit his friends in ones, twos at most. The guests were nice: variations on Bruce's taste for gentleness and responsibility. For me the gathering had a soft, disheveled quality but maybe for Bruce it rivaled the hectic party in *Alice in Wonderland* where all the characters converge and act characteristically.

If there was a Red Queen, she would have been Martin, a famous art historian and Marxist critic who really wielded some French majesty. A group of young men gathered around Martin; he was larger, large featured, but then he increases in the memory. He was glad to be back from Edinburgh; he had delivered a paper at a Poussin symposium. 'In San Francisco,' he said, 'winter is the follower of spring, summer and autumn; in Scotland winter is the long reform movement after a frivolous adventure.' Martin dispensed the last word on many subjects but not to us; nevertheless our heads bowed thoughtfully in intense feudal obeisance (waiting for the axe) or cocked, modern and ironic (the axe already passed through). An attractive young man proffered an insight: 'It is part of a general feeling in the modern world that life has become abstract,' he said hopefully. Martin smiled benignly. During the Reign of Terror the executioner on his scaffold sometimes held a head

aloft, alive for sixty seconds of consciousness if it
didn't go into shock, and showed the head its dead
body. OH MY GOD, THERE'S MY BODY A
USELESS OBJECT I'M DEAD THE COMPLETE
HORROR OF . . . I learned that from a movie named
Wolfen, a new age werewolf film with a message. One
topic was as good as the next but the movies provided
a Rorschach test so that anything could be discussed.
Wolfen tells us that the world is divided into good and
evil, and that evil is rich white people. We agreed
about some things and disagreed about others. Were
the monsters real or metaphorical? Martin explained
how they were symbolic but his argument, although
beautiful, proved to be such a baroque cathedral that
I lost faith, and besides, the strain of wearing my
contacts, a little French T-shirt and jeans, together
with a few gin and tonics, all in preparation for Jack,
made me feel slightly glassy. We agreed that the
movie was upsetting because it insisted on images of
decomposition. In the forensic lab a cadaver is trans-
ferred from a metal gurney. A hand that had fallen
bonelessly over the edge must be jerked to release its
hold, and we see it frozen in its position as nails scrape
across the stainless steel surface. More frightening
than dead flesh was the utter desolation of the movie's
locale, the South Bronx: earth robbed of increase and
joy. It looked like the moon, like a shattered war zone,
like the End—a rent in the fabric of daily life more
alarming than a monster or a corpse. No wasteland is
more grueling. It made Eliot's landscape resemble

37

Leave It to Beaver's neighborhood. Our lives resist artistic production; there is either an Auschwitz of meaning or a Farrah Fawcett vapidness that goes to the bone.

We talked about another movie, *An American Werewolf in London*. Bruce, Denise, my mother and I had seen it together a few weeks earlier. My mom was visiting for a week. She is a reserved, elegant woman and despite the collective impression she makes of a well-stocked pantry, she likes outré movies, science fiction and horror, perhaps because these movies conjure a time when good and evil were clearer. After the film we returned to my flat and defrosted some Hungarian pastry my mother had baked. In an afternoon she recreates both our childhoods and also the Austro-Hungarian Empire out of chocolate, walnuts, raisins, flour, eggs, sugar, vanilla and poppy seed. My mother says she likes almonds but not almond flavor like marzipan. I say I do. She says *See?* abbreviating the sad wisdom of the ages: two people are different. The differences exclude each other—and the people? She cracks an egg and pulls it apart with her thumbs, breaking its shell into halves; some white spills into the bowl; she pours the remaining egg back and forth between the half-shells, letting more of the white spill each time until she has only the yolk. Two people are different: the first source of wonder—both of us feel relief and regret.

While she kept to the liturgy of measuring, mixing, kneading, waiting, kneading, rolling, shaping, preheating, baking and offering, I puttered around, gossiping with her, scaling and cleaning some little trout for our dinner. My mother likes trout; when she was a girl she caught them in streams around Leadville, Colorado. She would yank one out and then, tender hearted, say, 'Tsk, poor thing!' The trout made me uneasy, I couldn't draw a bead on how to feel toward them. One moment each distinct fish life would be authoritative. It's impossible to imagine being a fish shimmying through water without also being slightly aroused. In the pink gills, black and silver eyes and armored frowns I read the jolt into the swirling air, suffocation, and I felt the resonance and intoxication of killing an animal to eat. The bodies took their position from the edge of the sink or the bodies of other fish—slate gray glinting blue; they looked dead. Later in a dream I gaze down at the sink and counters—scores of fishheads cover them in an even layer. The fishheads are still alive, fish out of water, their silver jaws and red gills gasping mechanically: I hold my breath. They have tongues which wag with distress and their flat eyes tilt in all directions. I would writhe if a fishhead touched me; one touches me and I wake with a shout. It was Jack's hand on my thigh. He had been watching me sleep. He drew me to him and I folded myself into his body. Then again, the fish would lose their identity and cleaning them seemed as impersonal as opening a letter marked Occupant.

> 'Are you ready yet?' I asked the cake. 'In

about five minutes,' it replied. I served it with coffee and strawberries. It was an *arang galuska*, balls of sweet yeast dough rolled in apricot glaze and ground walnuts, then stacked in a bundt pan and baked. Our forks detached morsels and lifted them. Or one of us put the fork down and concentrated: the sweet blandness of the dough was the real triumph. When heated its loose texture inhaled warm air and released it as a yeasty perfume. The tart apricot kept our taste buds awake to this mildness, the slight crunch of the nuts alerted us to the cake's extreme tenderness. We shared coffee, strawberries and pastry, all of us tasting the same flavors.

'It's opulent,' Bruce said, 'like jewelry, a way of marking occasions with glamour and richness—really delicious.'

My mom smiled and tipped her face back a little as though he were praising her beauty. 'Most of us would settle for a diamond of less than superlative quality,' she replied, generalizing the compliment, 'but when it comes to pastry, why bother unless the results are stunning?'

We felt lively and relaxed. The werewolf was really brilliant we all agreed, a wonderful monster. *Life* had done a spread on it—the most authentic werewolf in memory. And its human shape, David, transformed Lon Chaney Jr.'s simpy whiner and complainer. David was a good looking smartass little Jew from New York. All his victims lingered in a zone of semi-death annexed from the neighboring vampire myth; they cropped up at odd moments in progressive stages of rottenness trying to persuade David to kill himself and end this particular strain of werewolf curse, releasing them into undivided death which looked pretty good from their point of view. Denise said her favorite moment in horror films is when the old doctor, the authority figure, finally agrees—thanks to a lot of facts and urgent convincing and a dusty parchment book full of evil engravings and Latin—that the solution lies beyond the pale of ordinary science, in a twilight where Maria Ouspenskaya, the ancient one, intones a gypsy rhyme by the campfire—*Even a man who is pure of heart*—where superstitions and rituals shrouded in antiquity are observed by quaint out-of-the-way villages on misty heaths when the wolfbane blooms: the peasants, tight-lipped and unfriendly, glance at each other knowingly when the moon is full and bright, except for one, a sorrowing mother who implores you not go out on the moors on this particular night but, if you must, at least take this cross (even if you're Jewish) for your mother's sake. Our notion of life and death is superficial. Scratch the surface and what do you have fermenting up from below waiting for its chance to seize our soulless modern assumptions by the neck? We stagger from the atavistic shock of recognition. Until now, we didn't know the *meaning* of suffering, remorse and tragedy. What's a little dark night of the soul compared to your one and only body rippling like a kid's drawing of waves, sprouting hair in odd places, fierce enlargements, terrible urges, explosions in the chest, panic and tears, hormones running wild—the anguish of unruly pleasures, low and keening like a dark wind. 'It sounds like puberty,' said Denise. 'I want my mama,' I replied and there she was, telling us a not very comforting story from her childhood in Leadville.

Mr. Springhetti was the father of Maxine, my mom's best friend. The Springhettis were Italian. My mother's family was Hungarian. In those days everybody was something; English was spoken with an accent when it was spoken at all, and stepping into the Springhettis' house was like entering a house in Florence, the framed saints, the big kettles, the noodles cut thick; while my grandmother's door opened on central Europe, the knobby mahogany furniture, the *paprikash*, the noodles cut thin. The Springhettis had four other children. Mr. Springhetti had a handlebar mustache and a dream in life: he wanted to bag a moose. But he was getting old and not in great physical shape. Maybe he had ulcers. He hunted less and less; slim chance of killing a moose. Yet one summer day he did find one; he aimed his rifle and shot it. Imagine his swoon of possession, his gratitude—still, scavengers would claim the carcass before long. There was little point to being a hunter if you couldn't display your moose and blab about it, so Mr Springhetti resolved to hoist it onto his horse. You have to figure how much a moose weighs. He heaved and exerted till finally he ruptured his body. He died shortly afterwards from internal injuries sustained dragging a moose across the Rockies. Mrs. Springhetti mounted the moose head and hung it in the dining room and from then on my mom always felt funny, chilled actually, entering that room, as though Mrs. Springhetti raised up an idol to worship. How could she let the cause of Mr. Springhetti's death replace him at the dinner table and oversee every meal for the rest of her life? As far as my mother was concerned, an equal sign united Mr. Springhetti and the moose, they murdered each other, or perhaps Mr. Springhetti shape-shifted into a moose in a werewolf transformation. 'They should have been buried together,' said Denise. The Springhettis didn't lack for money, my mom continued. He left Mrs. Springhetti the Hudson agency and the Shell gas station—and she went on to make even more. She left it all to Lewis, her alcoholic and only son, who promptly squandered it.

43

Mr. Springhetti was my mother's first dead person, decked out in his fancy coffin with his formidable mustache. She brought strawberries to the funeral supper.

'Strawberries?'

'When the berries ripened, strawberries, blackberries, blueberries, we would eat them day and night. We forgot about meals, we just ate berries from big wooden tubs filled with heavy cream.' A trance of berries, the cream turning pink or gray-blue or purple. I pictured this family taken into a ripeness and carried up. That was the most sensual fact my mother ever told me about herself.

**Back at the party we were still talking about
*An American Werewolf in London***

44   I REPLIED TO a question from Martin—
my favorite is when we meet an English couple the
werewolf mauls and then discards like junk food. In
life Judith and Harry were hopelessly trivial with the
worst chirrupy public school accent, always popping
off or carrying on, and the joke is that death does not
transfigure them, does not ennoble them or give them
access to an essence or a Truth or even a point of
view; the mystery and gravity of their position vis-à-
vis the Ultimate expresses itself in a fit of pique and a
death-is-a-knock-knock-joke giddiness. Bruce located
Judith and Harry in his favorite part: six or seven of
the undead sit around a desolate porno theater lobby-
ing David to commit suicide. Although most of the
audience is dead, the actors and actresses on the screen
are deeply absorbed in a sexuality that looks deader.

And where is the actual audience, us, Bruce asked, in this box in a box?

That's when Jack came in, two hours late, dressed in the good overalls and carrying a watermelon. He distributed first names and waved greetings with a surprised expression as though he were Beauty on a float, and his expression did not subside until I took the melon from him. I gave him a kiss. 'Why Jack, you have liquor on your breath.' I kissed him again. 'Not beer. Scotch?' Jack fixed me with tensed eyes, as though *I* were the mysterious one. Then he rubbed his chin and his gaze floated away. Maybe *any* personal question was a blunder? I made space for his watermelon on the buffet but it was a beached whale among the dips and finger food so we decided to save it for Bruce to eat later. In the refrigerator it did not look out of place or cumbersome among Bruce's food: yogurt and wheat germ and soy cakes and fresh peanut butter, brown bread from the People's Bakery and a lot of fresh vegetables. That left Jack and me alone in the kitchen.

'Well, Jack,' I began, 'it's nice to see you.' We stood face to face; I was stepping softly on the toes of his left foot. Jack had ignored me all week. I couldn't account for my attraction to someone with so little appetite; I felt nostalgic for a joy which I had projected in the first place. Jack's orgasms dominated my imagination, his glossy head thrown back, eyes half shut and the quick steps of his breath—on my belly drop white jets light and revolting as insects—I recoil as though they were whips and also welcome them with a *ha!* of victory. I imagined everyone's orgasms, men women old young, the voluptuous thrashing and positions and moans—higher or lower—that would be like them. Someone thrusts a tongue in an ear and the person squirms like a speared fish. More, I found these convulsed bodies and faces extremely moving in their sheer physicality, sensual and imperiled.

'See my teeth, Jack—even and white. Three years of orthodontics,' I murmured, wrapping my voice in silken veils of seduction.

Without missing a beat he said 'Beautiful teeth' and awarded them a lingering kiss.

'And a beautiful smile?' I hinted.

'A rosebud filled with snow?' Jack ventured.

'Oh pshaw,' I replied, a modest virgin.

I took Jack's hand. 'Feel my stomach, Jack.' I put his palm on my abdomen. 'One hundred sit-ups every morning.' Jack slid his hand around my waist, found my lower back and drew me to him.

Our music changed cadence with the change in body language. His hot whisky breath touched my ear, whispered, 'Your eyes are sapphires!'

'Ah Jack, you understand how sexual precious stones can be.'

'They flash with an inward fire.'

'That's right—' I was Ann Dvorak seducing George Raft with her shoulders and sinuous beauty, insinuating, insinuating, while downtown the Momma

Mia worries the white dough of Europe. We've been eating under neon EAT and SUEY signs but from now on it's going to be spats, testimonial dinners and control of the whole North Side. 'Jack, tell me more.'

'Your navel is like a round goblet; your nipples are two fawns, twins of a gazelle; your neck is a pillar of ivory; (here he glanced down meaningfully) it's like the Tower of Lebanon that looks toward Damascus.'

BOB: Very foxy stud, 34, 5'10", 145, Blue-Brown, seeks sensitive man for hot action.

JACK: To whet your appetite, this one's a 5'8", 140 lbs., 34, sensual touching, no beards or smokers.

BOB (vehemently): I wrote your name on every stone in Mexico.

JACK: At a soirée we ate pâté and soufflé served by valets in a chalet in a valley watching pliés by a—

BOB (pushing Jack away): I love you, Psychological Novel.

JACK: I want to run with you in slow motion naked through the waves on Big Sur coast—

BOB: Wander through the shops and museums of Manhattan on a crisp—

JACK: Dine in an offbeat—

BOB: Travel, moonlight, Italy—

JACK: A backpacking trip through high mountain passes to a remote alpine meadow where we sleep together, a blanket of a billion stars overhead framed only by the silhouette of craggy—

'That'll do, Jack.' My seduction scene was overproduced; it disappointed me. Lack of grounding was the price of our flexibility. Jack reacted as though I sought to establish my beauty as a fact. I could have drawn up a list proving the opposite just as easily. I wanted: *There are threescore queens, and fourscore concubines and maidens without number—my dove, my undefiled is but one.*

The refrigerator hum clicked off and its wave of silence surprised and dispersed us as though we had been held inside that noise against our will. It carried us out into the living room, the day shifted—more talk, hellos, embraces, wine in plastic cups.

Martin had grown ruddy and expansive; his gravelly voice organized the people who stood around him, transforming their ears into theoreticians. 'Take Greuze—he's the obvious turning point.'

Jack volleyed that back as a topic sentence. 'The turn that Greuze represents in French painting is epitomized by his relation to Chardin.' I was awed by Jack's finesse. 'It was Greuze,' he continued, 'who inherited the absorptive essence of Chardin. But the sentimentalism, emotionalism, moralism, exploitation of sexuality and invention of narrative-dramatic structures characteristic of Greuze make a sharp contrast with the concentration and purity of Chardin.' They talked and I stood back. Jack's two day growth, black curls, overalls and flannel shirt lent a colloquial tone to his discourse but there was no mistaking its brilliance. To my surprise Martin steered a corn chip loaded with guacamole toward Jack's face—it was already on course when Jack saw it, so near his eyes crossed. My lips parted as it entered him. I felt a welling up of love; Jack obviously impressed and excited Martin. They traded phone numbers. The French Eighteenth Century was Martin's subject—Chardin, Greuze, Fragonard; he wanted a later meeting, an 'in-depth' discussion. Then Jack went to greet a friend, a tree-trimmer. For a moment we considered Jack's rear. Gloating with possession I said, 'It's a choice ass.' Martin piously countered, 'He's a very beautiful man.'

I talked with Cyrus, a young poet who won a national talent search by a New York press which was publishing his first book. He based it on ancient **49** Japanese themes. Cyrus was handsome and smart; he dressed stylishly; he was 'high yellow' from New Orleans, with almond eyes and eyelashes like a llama. Bruce liked him and I did too although after twenty minutes about his book and travels and friends and plans, when Cyrus finally did ask me a question about my life, it stood out so baldly, so lacked conviction that he turned the question into a joke. I introduced Jack to Cyrus and they settled in for the next hour.

They sat on facing director's chairs in the exact center of the party, talking soulfully in a tête-à-tête that recast the rest of us as ignored weather, and we agreed to be dull in order to highlight those two. I overheard Jack say, 'Americans get all worked up when they see *Roots* and *Holocaust* but the fact that our tax dollars finance the same shit in El Salvador is page ten news.' Cyrus nodded. They were vaguely disappointing from an eavesdropper's point of view. But during their long rapport there was some sincere pressing of hands, knees were certainly caressed. Cyrus was beginning to see himself on a larger scale. His conversation deepened, shimmered. When Jack spoke it was about Cyrus; Cyrus's forehead furrowed, two silky ripples in an ecru tablecloth. They exchanged numbers. Cyrus wanted to part with Jack so the pleasure of their reunion would open them inside out like Japanese paper water flowers, so that even their personalities grew floral, lacquered pinks and lavenders, perfectly knitted and pleasantly diverse, swaying in time at the end of stems and stalks like two thousand years of tradition, part of some harmonious continuum that ends with a comfortable little palace for Jack and Cyrus in, say, the two hundred and fiftieth heaven, not the most resplendant, the suburbs really: Jack comes home after a hard day of theatrical weather; 'Holiday for Strings,' all pizzicato, sets a perky mood as Cyrus does the last of the tidying up—Jack surprises him from behind—putting a spice cake in the oven—crinkle of embroidered silk—cool breeze—Jack penetrates Cyrus (they are elemental urges) and rocking together they comprise a golden principle of unity as their cake becomes spicier and spicier.

The sky looked bruised, and that's the way the air felt, achey

ON THE WAY home I asked Jack about **51**
Cyrus. Low tranquil clouds made the sky a ceiling only slightly higher than the one we'd just left.
It was getting to be twilight, the dull resonance of space like two rows of improbable cypresses, extravagant foliage depicted in a perspective into which Jack and I were drawn. Jack said, 'I think he's nice.'

'What constitutes his niceness?' The silence was a long organ note.

Jack retreated, he looked lost. The liquor had worn him out. He ran his fingers through his curls to dispense with me. His face was drawn, white showed around his irises and his sentences dropped. 'He's interesting.'

'How so? You mean you like his cock?' I

asked smiling, a crisp fan of malice opening to the full semi-circle.

'No, he's amusing.'

I looked to see if Jack were concealing his irritation; apparently there was none to conceal. His face read: polite interest, slightly bored. 'He *amuses* you, does he?' I snorted. 'That's on the same scale as liking his cock.'

Jack didn't appreciate the extent of his wrongdoing and in fact neither did I. Cyrus *was* nice, interesting, amusing and I was boring even myself; I had lapsed into a part written for a moron; I was about two sentences away from 'I'll scratch his eyes out!' Jack fucks Cyrus—so what? I might have bickered with the twilight for its lack of resolution. Cyrus wasn't going to elope with Jack's heart any more than I was. We had projected ourselves into Jack at two hundred miles per hour but he had not been there to catch us. Jack, where are you?

Asleep. While I showered, preparing for a festival of the senses, having had enough for a while of love's festival of meaning, Jack took off his overalls and pulled up my narcissus sheets and started breathing regularly at once. I thought of Joe-Toe. As Joe-Toe I climbed up the ladder of Jack's breath into bed, thinking, 'Anyone who really knew Joe-Toe knew that lying on his right side meant masturbation. For Joe-Toe, sleep was left handed.' Pieces of male bodies replaced each other on my mind's screen, like bath-house ads, muscular thigh, veined belly, lower back ropey and intricate, ass smooth naive exploitable: fuck me, I am drenched with water, darkness and availability. Jack rolled over. Without opening his eyes he said, 'Let me look at your torso.' After a moment he continued, gesturing theatrically with his perfect hand. 'When I jilt you . . . or when you jilt me . . . or we both dump each other . . . don't feel bitter, or frozen, or "knocked up." I can see by looking at you that you like to fuck and suck.' Then he resumed his steady breath. He was saying that to Joe-Toe, I guessed.

    'Why should I suffer?' I thought glumly. I got out of bed and went to the baths. There I did find pieces of bodies, several bodies in fact. They didn't want to chat with me or read the *Chronicle* together or watch *Charlie's Angels* on TV—well, neither did Jack, he hated the ordinary. But they did want to fuck. One man eased his cock into my ass. My asshole went from opaque to transparent as he lifted me off the floor and fucked me slowly with authority while another blew me and occasionally took my balls in his mouth while still another tongued my nipples and kissed me and many others touched my body lightly as though they were sensual Greek breezes. I recalled a heavy-set man at the baths who stood getting fucked and blown. His partner rammed him and broke the code of no words with shouts of *fuck* and *shit* while the chunky man gazed down modestly at the blow job. Was he embarrassed or completely absorbed, concentrating on his insides? Impossible to tell. His thick body seemed amazingly stable given the violence of the thrusts. My body was held in place. When I realized that I relaxed backward, releasing my ass and letting my head loll—the man fucking acknowledged my shift with a whispered *ha* that seemed triumphant. Men stood around, serious, watching us as I had gravely watched the chunky man. We watch the pleasure rather than the men, feeling the potential interchangeability. One of them masturbated me, others tended me respectfully because the one who is fucked induces awe by his extreme exposure. To look someone in the eye or call out his name would have been intrusive: their collective mind said *he's doing it* which my finite mind repeated. Although they masturbated themselves to obtain immediate knowledge of my excitement, it was as spectators that they solemnly shared in what my pleasure revealed. In the first place I was naked, their eyes and hands on my body confirmed that. In the second place I was desired. In the third place I was penetrated, which put me in a class by myself. The hand on my cock short-circuited pain, vouchsafing the more resonant pleasure from the cock in my ass—resonant pleasure, eager ass. *Do that* I said mentally. Complexity dropped away. I was set, things were settled—I felt a soldier's fidelity to the orgasm now that it was singled out from all the orgasms in the flux. The purely physical deepened, or rather became more incisive, more pressing, relegating any previous terms as though I were a body torn into existence. I, my identity, was more and more my body so I/it cried out with each released breath, not to express myself but as a by-product of physical absorption. But the spasms that were not me overtook and became me along with a sense of dread. I felt like a tooth being pulled. I covered my eyes and laughed once with excitement and dismay; I yielded to the gathering fullness with shame as though I pissed thinking *everyone can see me*, and glanced down with confusion at my sperm.

Getting fucked and masturbated produces an orgasm that can be read two ways, like the painting of a Victorian woman with her sensual hair piled up who gazes into the mirror of her vanity table. Then the same lights and darks reveal a different set of contours: her head becomes one eye, the reflection of her face another eye and her mirror becomes the dome of a grinning skull/woman/skull/woman/skull—I wanted my orgasm to fall between those images. *That's not really a place.* I know. The pious Victorian named his visual pun 'Vanity.' I rename it 'Identity.' I relinquished the firm barrier that separated us—no, that separated me from nothing. I might have liked to shoot far for boundlessness but when I get fucked in the ass that rarely happens, it just spills.

A part of me that was always busy was now totally at rest. I closed my eyes from intensity. A driving storm of new wave music beat four four against the silence. My eyes opened randomly on dramatic tableaus circled by darkness like the passionate kiss illumined by a flash of lightning in a Victorian

novel, darkness parting before that embrace and join-
ing after it—

: a waist arching calls attention to the nipples
and sends the smooth ass backward giving access—
someone slowly kneels

Two mouths, four nipples, four hands, two cocks, two

: the shifting of buttocks

scrotums, two assholes, two hundred and sixteen possi

: one excited man excites others to a circle of
masturbation—hands and cocks group and regroup
like a sudden wind shifting a garden, or like a story:
when a cock comes it withdraws from the plot

bilities and then another man joins you—an orgy in the

: someone is fucking a face he can't see, slow
rhythmical ass that opens out and then clenches, its
dreamtime logic has a unity that can't be dismissed or
broken into parts, another man gazes contemplatively
at that ass, his mouth slack, his face inches away

dark: shocking in the anticipation and memory, its

: someone begins climbing a set of moans
that ends in orgasm, he will thrash unless someone
holds him firmly by the shoulders

dreamtime logic has a unity that can't be dismissed or

: a bead of saliva on a nipple or cockhead
catches all the light, retains it for a second and then
forgets it

broken into parts, a basic human experience while it's

: naked men standing or sitting on ban-
quettes, adding a necessary quotient of boredom and
potential

happening—sex as a consciousness altering state—yet the
        : a man on his hands and knees, another man
milks him like a cow—the sperm comes—a low *huh*
from the spectators
experience is limited to so few; in the first place a gay orgy
        : a man *kneels*
is feared as unnatural; in the second place a gay orgy is
        : a man stands feet apart slowly masturbat-
ing and gazing at a man who masturbates standing
feet apart and returning that gaze
feared as too natural.

        : a belly and chest with come on it—we re-
spect that—a finger draws a line from nipple to groin

        Desire is not satisfied; it's *expelled*. Still, each
time pleasure was wrung out of me it seeped back   **57**
again and saturated my membranes. I should have
gone home, staying seemed greedy, but my orgasm
left me with more libido than before. To embrace
body after body—a deck of shuffled face cards which
you deal or discard—can have more resonance if
choice and chance express the times. Go where no
meaning is to create meaning. Take pleasure with the
abruptness of deities. Or Fred Astaire and Ginger
Rogers, their first dance not less stunning because it
doesn't include a home in the suburbs.

        A man passing grazes my right nipple; he
hears my gasp and returns interested. He traces a
voluptuous circle around the nipple; a line of feeling
shoots into my chest like the smell of gasoline. He
looks at my face hard, meaning he means it, then at

the nipple. First there's a membrane that wants a caress: the rest is history. Do I describe his face?—two dots and a line. He's giving me an erection—that interests him. I asked my dad about nipples and he said yes, that's why he always wears cotton T-shirts, even cotton irritates them. During puberty I could make myself come by caressing my nipples if toward the end I laid one finger on my cock. The man who is interested tongues my left one; it makes a hot entrance into his mouth and then he sucks the hard tip in and out gently and patiently between his teeth: it causes air to rush through me. I fondle his hair and ears, I love him so much I would do anything he asked me to, my arms are weak. His thumbnail lightly skirts the tip of the right one again and again; pleasure sets up the roll of a snare drum in my teeth, in the membrane under my cockhead and around my asshole—pleasure so aggressively familiar it registers as an affront and my chest is about to cry or shout out as though deeply refusing again and again increasingly released. The erect tip, faded pink, my nipple's leader, stands out against its rose circle; it has become the farthest point of me; sometimes when I eat chocolate my nipples get hard and the hairs around them stand up. I always admired nipples like Jack's—two dimes casually dropped on a table—my own are such peonies. When this man pinches and kneads and mistreats them—I always knew he was a heartless beast, they *act* like they love you, sure, and you end up bruised and sore—the sensation was confined to

my nipples and I negotiated the pain into an even
stronger and more telling happiness.

Naked men move swiftly even when we're
standing still, fluent passage from corridor to corridor
with orgasm as the only stop. Certainly the passage of
time is different when perceived with the whole body.
So many men: patterns of stress, dark and absorptive,
hardly differentiated from our surroundings. So little
time: actually no time, opaque instants where being
alive is form and content. To approach that instant we
move so swiftly we set up a high distracting turbulence
and push into it, squinting eyes and parting lips. Calm
becomes tedious and unbalanced, insupportable, the
body meets it with a shout of indignation.

And shouldn't Fred and Ginger ditch the
interior life that intimacy is based on? It's a brontosau-
rus, a vestigial organ longing for an appendectomy.
We are modern, sleek, with an arched waist echoed
by huge Deco arcs to an infinity of longing. Then the
music fades and Fred lights up, complacent, reducing
the encounter to performance and technique, a public
means of expression. A wail of protest goes up:
sensitive nipples, tender skin on the inner thigh—the
knowledge of which *equals* intimacy—what happens
to these secrets once I have shared them with so many
Freds that I am a machine whose quirks and eccentric-
ities are appraised in a cheerfully businesslike way? If
I'm so dispersed, what happens to the possibility of
intimacy for me?

I haunted the halls and dark places of the

59

Club Baths feeling less and less physically present. I had an upset stomach. My stock was plummeting. Everyone rejected me except for the people I rejected. An older man took my cock and I turned away, creating of him a blind spot but letting my cock face forward in case he wanted to give me pleasure. Instead he touched my chin, lightly turning my face toward him, and whispered, 'Smile, you look scared and sad.' I laughed with relief and embraced him and whispered, 'You're right.' I was glad he'd broken my stereotyped response—he moved on—I might have liked him to stay but he had already made his distinctions. I felt relief and regret.

Finally in a big dark room on the second floor someone grabbed my cock and got it hard. I took hold of his cock and recoiled—it had warts. He abruptly swung around and shoved my cock in his ass, then turned us both around so he could balance himself on the edge of a platform that held a mattress. His ass was wide open and lubricated with the sperm of untold others—I don't know more about him—he was shorter and he had a waist. I scooted him onto the mattress and fucked him; I figured his ass was a crock pot for every disease known to man. His body spun like a pinwheel on a stick. When I finished he didn't bother turning around to his past to reminisce, he just went forward looking for his next cock. I showered and each subsequent activity took me closer to home. I mentally started a bitter quarrel with Jack that continued for a year.

Jack was still breathing; the room smelled like burnt dust from a heater that had not been used in a long while. I shut the bedroom door. In the bathroom the white cotton rug cast the same narrow shadow on the dappled tile as the continent casts on the ocean. I saw it from outer space (the toilet seat)— 'as though he didn't live here' I explained in someone else's voice. On the way out a glance at the mirror advised me not to get too dramatic. Then I sat down abruptly on the stairs in the hall 'as though he suddenly remembered something' the voice continued. I cried mentally a few minutes, then climbed into the guest bed in my office. Lily tagged along, glad to have me back home. She curled into the blue mohair armchair, rested her chin on the arm and sighed deeply, regarding me with half-shut eyes of inexpressible dog weariness. It was about three in the morning, too tired for sleep. I watched five minutes of TV. A tall gangly man was getting into a little box. He started out by putting his leg behind his head and turning his body around so that his chest was in back of him and his foot up beside his head. Then he was ready to enter the box. First a leg, then the head, then a foot, then the other leg, and then he was inside. His assistant closed the lid and walked away; the man was supposed to remain in the box for thirty-seven minutes. I flipped the dial. Marlon Brando, in a fake English accent, was Napoleon Bonaparte. In a garden which Marlon's Schlitz beer voice dubs 'charming' in some ultimate perversity, he asks Jean Simmons if she

61

believes in DESTINY. She laughs. 'You laugh at DESTINY?' She replies, 'I was taught to laugh a lot.' I punched the off button; Jean and Marlon toppled backward into the screen in blue chemical decay. Lily, assuming her place as the helping animal of folklore, released a heartfelt sigh of contempt and beamed me a motto on the vanity of human wishes.

Then the bark of a neighbor's dog snapped her to attention; cocked ears belied her earlier cynicism. She growled and rumbled in an aggrieved whisper, then blurted out one fully articulated woof. The excitement over, she arched her tan back and slowly drew herself out of the chair; every vertebra from the base of her skull to the tip of her tail received its due. She climbed on the bed bringing with her the welcome odor of warm sweaters. She stretched out beside me, put her paw in my hand, her chin on my thigh, and gazed into my eyes. First her gaze amused me and I returned it. We searched each other for comprehension until I felt estranged from the bed and the big ugly desk and armchair and the friendly cardboard boxes filled with papers and projects. Her tan and chocolate eyes gathered up all the intelligent familiarity in the room. She continued to meet my gaze. It made me nervous. Minutes passed solidly, each the subject of itself. I tickled a certain spot between her front legs that for some reason induced a rear leg to pump mechanically and her tongue to loll until she was merely a dog. But when I finished she replaced her paw in my hand and resumed her expression of high inquiry—one apricot ear raised like an eyebrow—until her eyes filmed over, her eyelids grew heavy, and rocked by her own breathing she drifted off to sleep.

Sleep was growing more and more improbable, the losing side of a debate. Imagine a happy thing. Imagine yourself comfortable and at home and your body will step through that narrowing door. Imagine sleep as a door to step through, a field to fall in, a treetop to rock in, a chair to sink in, a hammock to swing in, a car to ride in, a horse to sit on. I could have slept if it rained. The room jolted and shifted through the darkness like a boxcar; reflected headlights swept across the ceiling, climaxing the mounting approach and quick subsiding of stranger's engines that gave away their motion to my room. 'Comfortable and at home' seemed like journey's end, porchlight on, the surprising familiar smell, smell of familiarity that can be acknowledged only for a moment—longed for and unifying—before it's too close to distinguish from the self. One sleepless night my mother said, 'Think about happy things.' She sat down on the edge of my bed with a tired exhaling sound. That sigh added to my list of worries—I did not want to outlive her. She was anxious to get away, to enjoy herself, worn out after a day of children, fearing the expense of a demand for intimacy. My sole drawing card was misery. *Happy things?* I pressed her—what specifically did she have in mind? Apparently she also drew a blank (there I felt we were united) because she finally

63

replied Mickey Mouse. I thought the answer dismissive and contemptible—did she think I was going to trade real misery for a cartoon mouse? I loved her more than anyone and I assumed she loved me that way: I *still* want her love, it's a design as structural in me as grain in wood, an imprimatur. Didn't she know me at all? If she didn't know me, who did? She was treating me like an abstract child: I was set adrift.

In my adult bed I started thinking about Mickey Mouse. My mother used to sing us his song from a 30's cartoon and I wondered what part the happy-go-lucky melody played in her child life under a high thin sky in that remote household of polished dark floors and rose carpets. Mickey's song challenged my assumption that my mother and I were the same. She was a tomboy, outgoing and tough. In the family album there's a photo of her—she must have been seven or eight—a mop of curls and one raffish foot on the running board of a stolid black seven-passenger Hudson limousine parked in an upland meadow, looking alien as a Victorian sofa and (like my mom) built to last. My mother carries a rag doll; it's tucked in the crook of her arm with the same lyrical nonchalance a boy might pay his catcher's mitt. Extreme self-consciousness corrupted me. My childhood needed many secrets and secret places to lend depth to my loneliness but at heart I was totally prosaic about my suffering and its attendant strategies of goodness and solitude; it was like standing in line at the bank for x number of years. To be so unhappy was humiliating;

64

I'll make a much better adult, I consoled myself. I listened to my breathing and waited to grow up.

> Oh I'm the guy they call
> Little Mickey Mouse.
> Got my sweetie down
> In the chicken house:
> Neither fat nor skinny
> She's the horses' whinny,
> She's my little Minnie Mouse—

So far so good; a ballad in Mouse falsetto. With a few deft strokes Mickey proposes as desirability itself the beauteous Minnie, Beatrice to his Dante—not fat, not skinny, Mickey characterizes the shapely mouse (in a daring leap from mouse to horse) as a whinny, a low and gentle neigh, perhaps a call or greeting that presages further developments in the song. These terms of respect and admiration do not mask the possessive nature of Mickey's attachment. Minnie is a sweetie that Mickey has 'got'; he sings, 'She's *my* little Minnie Mouse' (italics mine). We may condemn Mickey's patriarchal attitude toward women, or we may simply note the generic use of possessives in romantic ballads. But I would like to suggest a third interpretation: Mickey and Minnie are so meshed, so unified in their love that they literally do belong to each other and use the possessive with the same authority as, say, Tristan and Isolde. Mickey is not insensitive or unconscious but merely responds to a fact, indeed the

65

central fact of his existence. As we shall see, the remainder of the song favors this last construction.

But to digress a moment: as I recall Mickey sings his tribute while steering a ship up a river. This ship captain has a strangely bucolic image bank, typified by chicken houses and horses. Perhaps Disney wanted to include many walks of life in the figure of Mickey in order that his experience appear 'universal'; perhaps Disney wanted to set the rapture of the Mouses' interior lives against the awkward social realism of their trades. But Mickey makes the boat toot and whistle, he transforms it into a wind and percussion instrument; the landscape is not unwilling, it can be pummeled and drawn out like taffy, trees shimmy and spasm, the banks of the river heave and convulse with sympathetic vibrations. (The conventional French seventeenth century made a map of the land of love, *La Carte de Tendre*. My map includes Jack's apartment, Leadville, Colorado, and the Mouses' River and Farm.)

MICKEY: When it's feeding time
        For the animals
        They all howl and growl
        Like the cannibals,
        But I turn my heel
        On the hen house squeal
        When I hear my little Minnie—

MINNIE: Yooooo Hooooo

So Mickey and Minnie transcend the exigencies of commerce, which Mickey characterizes as the

Together they tread down the bourgeois insect that feeds on the life of the people (p. 76).

From a Russian Revolutionary Poster.

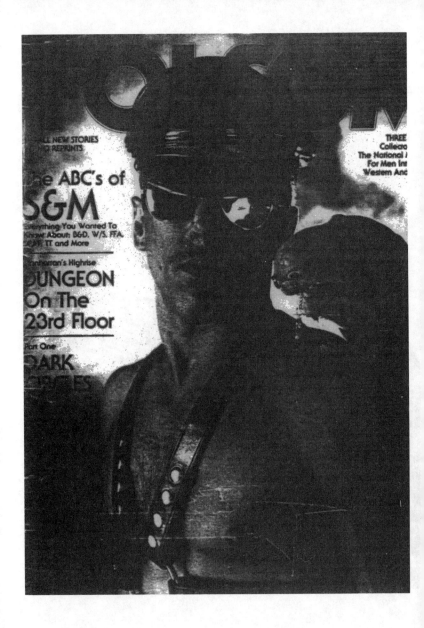

I lick my forefinger and touch the nipple (p. 86).

Folsom Photo by Jim Moss.

'howl and growl' of cannibals (a racist image in keeping with Disney ideology). The whole getting and spending world weighs less than Minnie's call to love. In the figure of Mickey we recognize Count Mosca from *The Charterhouse of Parma*, a man whose informing quality is capability, an intelligent man who creates a brilliant career, yet comprehends that power is a bauble. As easily as a light finger on a chin pivots a head, passion turns him away from his past and present; he abandons them in a simple gesture toward happiness when he hears his love's preemptive Yooooo Hoooo. This is Minnie's first entrance—how beautiful she is, with her eyelashes and stylish shoes. She shakes out her truck garden like a blanket; fertility. Now we see that Minnie is the root of Mickey's *Georgics*; and for Minnie speech is about rivers? Everything comes alive for them—communication sails forth—the world is at hand when Minnie Yooooo Hooooos in wild rapport.

67

About two hours later the phone rang, waking me up

IT WAS MY friend Tom, shitfaced. He sounded as though he had been drinking for a long time. He was crying—he was in despair. His cells were drenched in alcohol and I recognized a liquor pain that turned his body into an unhappy X, an extremity of crossed circuits that could have generated, had he been happy, an exhilaration just as wrenching.

'Don't hang up on me, Bobby—I try and it doesn't make a difference. I want to make a difference.

'I want to be touched—I can't fucking believe it—I'm in the bar—I always liked the person—he's going crazy. I say, There's NO *reason* why you should *do* this. I just couldn't talk to him. You won't hang up will you?'

'No sweetheart, I'm not going to hang up.'

'I just couldn't talk to him. But he came

back and came back and he just kept coming back. Then I would dispossess him. Are you there?' His voice was strained and exhausted.

'You should go to sleep, Tom.'

'I would turn him away like I've always turned people away. I want to die. That comes right out of the middle of my heart. It's like living through a scene that comes up through your body—'

Tom wailed with despair. A howl of despair.

'I love you. I care for you so much—blue eyes and all that white skin. You're the bright one in the family, I'm the one with the heart—do something with all this unhappiness—Don't hang up on me.'

I said I wouldn't and that I loved him. I said it again but it didn't register. I told him to get some sleep.

He said, 'I am all-devouring. I want someone to give me all their energy. So I can turn it into ideas.' Then the phone clicked and without transition I was alone.

DENISE: Hello?
BOB: Hi. It's me.
(The scrape and rush of a match and Denise inhaling.)
BOB: Nancy Reagan was on a L.A. game show where you put your hand in a box and identify a certain object by touch. First a screen lights up and lets the studio and the TV audience know—so it lights up

and spells out with hundreds of tiny bulbs the words DONKEY DICK. Nancy puts her hand in the box, then asks the moderator, 'Is it edible?' The moderator answers, 'Well, I guess so—uh, yes.' Nancy replies, 'Donkey Dick?'

DENISE (blurted): Hahahahaha. (pause) That's sick.
(She says the latter with such finality that Bob wonders if she recalls laughing one second before.)

BOB: I went to the baths last night.

DENISE: You usually have fun at the baths.

BOB: Mixed reviews—I knew before I went it was going to be difficult. The last time was really awful—I couldn't get an erection.

DENISE: Then why did you go?

70 BOB: I needed sex.

DENISE: Needed?

BOB: If I don't have sex every week or so I feel out of kilter and hysterical. Don't you?

DENISE: No. Are you ruled by your body?

BOB: Well, yesss . . . I hope so. What else?

(Pause)

DENISE: Your mind.

BOB: My mind. Are you?

(Pause)

DENISE: Yes.

(Both backtrack.)

DENISE: Your mind's in your body.

BOB (musically): Noooooooooo. It's about half way between my body and the world.

DENISE: So your body rules?

BOB: Let's say it's a constitutional monarchy.
DENISE: Where was Jack?

TOM: Hello?
BOB: Hi, it's Bob. How are you?
TOM: Bobby, I really don't know the kindest way to break this: dead. Remember last night when I called everyone up—even LaPorto in Chicago and Zeb in New York—and no one would talk to me? Now I'm in heaven where God has me answering phones. He's just like that song from the 60's—When you see him coming you better step aside.
BOB: A lot of men didn't and a lot of men died.
TOM: Big John. God doesn't like Cha-Cha. Anyone special you'd like to talk to?
BOB: You Tom, I'd like to talk to you.
TOM:
BOB: OK. John Keats.
TOM: Bobby, he's in the Other Place.
BOB: Hans Memling.
TOM: Other Place.
BOB: Lots of elbow room up there.
TOM: We're four, if you count God three times.
BOB: What's it like?
TOM: Like being all alone in Saks, like being worn by a Calvin Klein shirt.
BOB: Calvin Klein?
TOM: The Lord appreciates good design.
BOB: Are you happy?
TOM: Are you kidding?

BOB: Want to resurrect?
TOM: Bobby.

BOB: Hi. I went to the baths last night.
BRUCE: Which one?
BOB: The Club.
BRUCE: And?
BOB: I had a great time 'til I had a bad time. I guess I stayed too long. By the end I felt like Nancy Reagan in Jack's donkey dick joke.
BRUCE: Someone at the baths in Portland told me that, but instead of Nancy Reagan it was Queen Elizabeth. It was funnier, more apropos the refinement, the horsey set.
BOB: Did you have fun?
BRUCE: Let's see. Going in, a guy smiles at me and I smile back—later I'm at the door to his room but not inside, we're just exchanging two or three sentences—but then somebody comes along, butts in front of me, and as the door slams in my face I deduce that that is not the place for me.
BOB: Hummmmm.
BRUCE: Then I'm getting cruised by this total superman. That seems very strange to me but it turns out I'm exactly who he has in mind. But he just wants jerk off, macho-buddy sex and it's not turning me on. I tell myself I should be excited: here's a commodity gay fetish legions of gay men would give an arm and a leg etc. He's an art student at Berkeley but sort of a surfer upstairs. So while I'm sitting beside this one

point seven carat diamond I keep thinking, shouldn't I wear him in my tiara? Then things explain themselves a little. Part of the reason for my lack of desire is his lack of relation to his own body. His father brutalizes him, refers to him as 'that faggot.' So there's this element of non-sexuality.

BOB: What did he look like?

BRUCE: Like Superman. Like ten hours a week in the gym. A real Anglo. So then I wander around a bit more. I see a guy lounging with a cigarette. He smiles, I smile—warm vibes, nice looking. I pass him without stopping, then he goes to his room. I backtrack and ask for a cigarette—this is wonderful because I love cigarettes and sex. I ask if he'd like to smoke and talk, and after a while we touch each other.

BOB: What does he look like?

BRUCE: He's about six feet, about an inch shorter than I am. But what's really interesting is how his body is developed, a physical illustration of economy and flexibility. On touching him I find an extreme muscularity but not at all like bodybuilding. In bodybuilding your chest is rounded almost like a woman's, but his is flat and hard—so I ask myself, what is it?

His eyes are brown, he's very white looking, his face has a roundness, a sculpted quality—'salt of the earth.' He reminds me of the working class men of the Northwest, when white meant working class, particularly in Portland with its German and Scandinavian immigrants, loggers and brewers. So that's what he plugs into.

I don't think I ever had a more smooth and flexible and tactful and unobtrusive introduction to lovemaking.

BOB: Once I was lying on a platform in a big room at the Sutro Baths and a black guy walked toward me— very slowly, naked. His cock was level with my head. He walked like the roll of a snare drum—very drawn out. When he was right in front of me I reached up to his hip and lightly pivoted his cock into my mouth. We made love for hours; we seemed to have identical rhythms. Even anonymous sex has a huge range of commitment to a partner and to fucking.

BRUCE: That's right. There was an informing sense of rhythm and something mental that supposed I would be alert to needs and wants and that he would be the same. And a further revelation in that our bodies were in such good shape, so finely attuned— there was a physical base to this ability to respond. I had just trained for the marathon, with all that that entails.

In everything we did there was a sense of reciprocity and equals—that's not the way sex characteristically happens for gay people or straight people, but maybe everyone hungers for it whether we know it or not.

So then after an hour we had another cigarette and then another hour of sex and then another cigarette and then another hour of sex.

BOB: Three hours you made love?

BRUCE: We were together for about six.

BOB: What's his name?

BRUCE: Edmund LaPlanche.

BOB: What does he do?

BRUCE: He's a rider.

BOB: He writes?

BRUCE: I made the same mistake. I said, 'I'm a writer too!' He rides horses. 'You must be rich or around a lot of rich people.' He said no and laughed and said but he used to be.

Ever since Edmund was a kid (in as he put it K Falls for Klamath Falls, which I really found attractive) he had ridden in competitions even in Europe, and he was a champion. After one European tour Paul Mellon offered him a job.

BOB: No! Of *the* Mellons? How rich?

BRUCE: In the top five or ten men. The Big Bucks. The Mellons are super ruling class because the family stayed small. Now there must be 3,000 DuPonts, so any given particular DuPont is only equivalent to a small town banker. Horses are one of Mellon's diversions. Edmund managed all Mellon's horse running operations, hunter-jumper and dressage training facilities, stables and shows. It was like being a valued servant. And Mellon's relation to his servants was every bit as caricatured as any cartoon millionaire. The first thing you do with a servant is break him, divest him of dignity so he'll know his place—and you pay him really a lot of money so that he will want to continue groveling. On the first day Mellon called Edmund to him by snapping his fingers and saying *boy*. Edmund gave him a dressing down, seeing what was at stake.

EDMUND'S SELF-RESPECT and Mellon's wickedness refreshed Bruce and me. Usually the rich are 'real people' like in *People Magazine* where they also have busy days, dilemmas, new boyfriends, etc. After all, the goal of many who live in the United States is to own it. But Edmund and Mellon reminded us of posters from Russia of 1917. Workers stride forward, red and black, the triumphant army of collective spirit, and in that stalwart contingent more than a few suck cock. Together they tread down the bourgeois insect that feeds on the life of the people; he's in his bowler, tux and spats and he carries an enormous cigar: power. He's fat and round, shaped like the world. The liberation army pushes him to the bottom left of the poster and off the stage of history. He tries to ward them off with the dead hand of the past but he sees his doom and his own evil heart—*evil heart* is too romantic, *savage depravity* too elevated—he's a murderous thug and slow death is too good (attack and disappear, attack and disappear). He really has killed people, maybe he's the puppet master of a Banana Republic or bankrolls a genocide, maybe he cooks up vicious little wars for peace and sells weapons to both sides. 'So,' says the capitalist, getting in the final word, 'I'm no longer master here. The cities rise up—a tide of darkness and revolt. The very ground I walk on tries to shrug me off. Look, the earth convul-

ses. I laid bare the purity of forms—always a religious
act. I invented the individual and the family—more
than a modest contribution. What beauty, what social
unit, what human being have you invented to match
these? I see my fall is twice determined: I am over-
thrown by the people, and also by my own inventions
which have grown cumbersome, ungainly, easy to tip
over. I assumed I was the world but in fact I'm a giant
zero!'

BRUCE: Edmund told me a lot of how-rich-is-rich
stories. The estate was in North Carolina and they
used to go often together to D.C. or New York.
Chauffeured? I asked. No chauffeur. *What, no chauffeur?*
Because he never used a limousine. *If no limousine,*
what? He traveled by helicopter. *What happens when*
there's no airport? Why, Mellon sends people ahead to
buy land and build a landing platform! And then
there's a lot of stories about world travel as a fact of
life. Edmund got more and more disgusted by rich
person stuff, being from a working class little redneck
town in Southern Oregon. And the money didn't
mean that much because Mellon kept giving him more
and more. The servility all around scared Edmund.

So Edmund gives notice. 'Paul, I'm going
on with my career, I'm giving you thirty days notice.'
Mellon says, contemptuously, 'I'll give you another
$1,000 a month.' Besides this money hook, Mellon
must have thought they had some kind of bond
because sometimes he talked intimately with

Edmund. Once Mellon talked about being rich: 'You know, Edmund, the nice thing about being rich'—and here I imagine his eyes narrowing and his jaw jutting out—'is you can do anything you want, anytime, any place—you can make anybody do anything you want.'

At different times during the thirty days Mellon comes up and says, 'Now for the World Championship at Burghley, the chestnut mare is good in cross-country, equitation, pleasure and hunter.' And: 'For the Arabian Nationals, El Gato is a three-day-event horse—I like his way of going in all three events, but the Arabian gelding—

BOB: Bruce?

78 BRUCE: So Edmund says, 'No Paul, you have it wrong I gave you notice I'm leaving at the end of the month.' Edmund is getting pretty worried. He packs his bags, goes to the airport, still worried, and there at the top of the escalator, barring the way, is *Paul Mellon*. Edmund says, 'Get out of my way, Paul, I'm leaving you.'

BOB: He said leaving *you*?

BRUCE: Yes.

BOB: That you is interesting: like a lover.

BRUCE: Or a child. Mellon puts his hands out on the escalator rails, blocking the way. 'No you're not.' 'Get out of my way Paul.' He doesn't. And then Edmund punches him and knocks him down and walks over him and doesn't even look back. He boards the airplane.

BOB: Jesus! What a wonderful story!
BRUCE: Edmund flew to the West Coast becoming more and more anxious. 'He could have his people waiting for me.' He didn't, but after all, he could have.

The funeral

I DROVE TO Kensington for a tree plant-
ing ceremony in Phyllis's backyard. I was late; the
afternoon shimmered with reflected heat; I felt
drugged, my head on crooked, my body excess bag-
gage. I stopped and looked through her screen door.
For an instant I looked through my family's screen
door with its scrolled aluminum G during a midwest-
ern summer twenty-five years ago. The screen bagged
and where it caught the sun I could see only white
texture but through the shadowed parts I saw in. I
tested her living room against my memory. Phyllis's
was casual and eclectic as though the attention she
paid it were a bit ironic; it held less evidence of a color
scheme or children and more books. I slipped into its
coolness and regrouped, then walked through the rest
of her house—a nice house in which feelings were

readily believable—and stepped down into the dazzling light. The ceremony had begun. I felt punch drunk from the heat. Poplars bordered the yard. Sunlight bleached the color out of the mourners, except for a crowded band in the poplar shadow which separated those who felt released by the full sun from those who felt besieged by it.

Musicians stood at the far side of the yard, a guitar and three singers. They had too many clothes on and heat blocked the sound; their hands moved across the strings and their mouths opened. The silence was only twenty feet deep but it pushed them away. Or perhaps my ears were exhausted—we wore attentive expressions. Then Phyllis kneeled and dropped his ashes in the hole. They set the tree in, and Phyllis and the other mourners watered it. *Then Phyllis changed into a stream bearing her name, which watered (with her tears?) the persimmon tree her son had become. Wild death, skin beneath bark, murmurous sorrow of the stream, the persimmon's red hearts: spirit informing grief making it nature.* The ceremony had no tradition to back it. There was no meaning to balance against Phyllis's loss, no way to look steadily at Peter's withdrawal from her present and future. Phyllis, diminished and stunned, was surrounded by a numb silence which gave her leeway to mourn but which she could not break out of—or am I transferring onto the mourner the qualities of the dead? I wondered if sorrow would be a link between herself and her son, the same kind of bond as anger or respect. The tree's roots were supposed to curl around the ashes but music and persimmon roots did not shape the grief and shock of the mourners.

Different people from Peter's life delivered short eulogies. I gathered he was about my age. Apparently he had been in some kind of trouble. It was my generation's usual: the giant public zero and enforced meaninglessness of the Viet Nam War and the excessive meaning (world in a grain of sand) conferred by drugs, so that meaning itself was seen as an ingredient, a prop along with the others to create an illusion—the plot, the backdrop, he said, she said—rootlessness that had you scrambling in the endless childhood Siberia of no immediate responsibility but guilt for everything. He lived in a state of peril. I imagine lies, then stress and more lies. Phyllis spoke, her hands clasped, then Peter's brother, father and girlfriend, and then a tall blond man who said with a hint of emphasis, 'We all loved him in our way.' He added that Peter had a great sense of humor. Soon they were repeating Peter's jokes. Many people had some story to add, the backyard came alive, we were laughing and the ceremony really did become beautiful. Earlier, Peter's death had challenged every value. Now the mourners were braiding him back into the community, so no wonder his metamorphosis occurred in the realm of language. These stories signaled Peter's public existence in the past tense, the beginning of the taming of his death.

Peter's humor was so wry and gentle that if

he had been in trouble I figured sweetness had led
him there. In a story from when he was seven, he and
his brother go trick-or-treating in bear costumes. One
neighbor asks, 'Shouldn't there be three of you?' Peter
looks up and mildly replies, 'Excuse me, sir, we're
happy as we are.' Together with the blond man's 'in
our way' and Peter's 'trouble' and his humor, I
wondered if he were gay.

Saturday began with a letter from Brian

IN L.A. TWO summers ago I had an affair
with Brian. I was moved and attracted but not really
in love, and Brian went on to another man who
offered him a full scale response. From this man Brian
kept one secret: me. Being a sin of omission flattered
and worried me. Maybe Brian harbored a passion that
his present lover could rightly resent as a present
claim rather than a prior one; Brian might see me as
part of his being that exists outside of his own power.
In the dark secret I had become, Brian hid a catalogue
of acts that made his memory resonate with criminal
sex viewed from a shocked averted glance: kneeling
bodies eagerly revamping the incestuous dramas,
allowing oneself to feel the terror that precedes worship, allowing oneself to be worshipped. But accord-
ing to this formula my actual self—the self that might

want to have sex with Brian again—did not figure in Brian's present; I was relegated to the past. Even his heroic image of me, radiant with projected joy, would yellow into an after-image and die away. Brian taught me what it's like to be loved without limits, love that glides and figure skates from geological distances to the cellular matrix, generating vast sensations of being permanently warmed and drenched to the bone at last. This is a gift of abundance I wish the same to you—why should we part with it?

I had wanted us to be friends. I should have known better. I almost laugh out loud when a man I've failed to secure proposes friendship. I'm on the phone in a Southern California sunset on a stucco porch. Along with the rest of L.A., I'm heating up and dehydrating from a steady Santa Ana wind. The stucco is peach colored and called something like Desert Twilight or Aztec Sand; birds of paradise surround the porch—fat, sultry flowers, orange and blue on thick pulpy stalks that insist on fertility. Maroon racing trunks distance and frame my crotch and patches of clamminess assert armpits and lower back. I sit on cool terra cotta steps with coffee cup and telephone—overhead hangs a rusty wrought-iron porch light with frosted glass panes whose pale glow takes on authority as a pink and green sky becomes night. I love L.A., it's always smiling for the camera. What did the world look like before the picturesque? Even in shots from space it's an object of contemplation without a hut to hide in. The globe's immobility, solitude, silence, all suspend time; I experience a pure and intense sensation of sweetness and the self-sufficiency of my existence—time no longer exists, nothing measures it. Earth continues in its sky like a nipple on the clear chest of a porn magazine. The model wears a leather harness and mirrored sunglasses that vaguely reflect his photographer, his human mirror; on his shoulder a parrot holds its chain in its beak; claws show us how easily the master's skin indents. The man's iridescent glasses, his chains and gorgeousness resemble the parrot in its inviting, remote beauty, and I wonder if the photographer intended that comparison. I lick my forefinger and touch the nipple. That's funny, I never thought that kind of activity would appeal to me. I'd be embarrassed if anyone *saw* me do that.

86

I picture Brian in Manhattan Beach or Laguna Beach or Redondo Beach or Pacific Palisades safe in his love nest: his lover hands him a tall sweating pink glass of one part vodka two parts Hawaiian Punch. Brian looks up and smiles his thank you, pats his lover's behind and says, 'Eat your heart out, Donny Osmond.' By sheer coincidence Donny's impossibly bland face surrounded by delighted Hawaiians appears on the portable Zenith they keep on the patio. The small fever of magazine color on the screen demands to be taken personally, as opposed to the dusky backyard. Donny seeks in our eyes the means to persuade us of his truth, then sings about Hawaiian Punch. The coincidence is so precise that

Brian suddenly feels like he's just smoked a lot of grass; he lies back on a chaise lounge of orange plastic and aluminum tubing, his eyes grow heavy and pleasure sets up a low voltage current in his joints and membranes. Brian is resting from an evening swim (here I manufacture for them a lozenge shaped pool). He wears white muslin shorts, very sheer, now wet and translucent, in which his cock looks like a ghost. Banana trees. Gold skin. Date palms. Dichondra. Pink and green sky. Blond hair and green eyes. A hillside of pastel houses that spills toward the double white line of freeway and beach. The phone rings.

'Brian, I don't want to lose you. I've been thinking about this a lot. I want to continue our friendship.' (Spoken with California sincerity on level one and baffled sexuality on level two and opportunism on level three *and so on.*)

'That's fine Bob, call me. I've got to go now. It's been real.'

'Remember when—'

'Bob, let's stroll down memory lane together some other time.'

That made sense to me from his point of view so I left him alone. But Christmas I got a card from him. The front showed a xerox image of Brian's new lover, Jerry, wearing sunglasses and suffering from high contrast—the wages of post-modernism. Brian, the apple of Jerry's eye, appeared reflected in his silver lenses. That message seemed pretty clear. Like the porn star and his photographer, they made a unit. Inside, beneath a constructivist dove towing with its beak the word *peace* in a sans-serif typeface, Brian had written *Brian*. *Brian* was the salutation, text and complimentary close. All January and February I kept the card by my place at the kitchen table and practiced an exegesis on that *Brian* while I read the morning paper.

It's wise to have a few distractions at hand when reading the *San Francisco Chronicle* since the only items of consistently high quality are the horoscope and Dear Abby, unless you're interested in the heart-broken families of Moonies or the long costly wait for organ donors. It discourages even a person like myself who relishes banality and assigns it to pleasure's most sophisticated department: acquired tastes. Abigail Van Buren's advice to STEAMED told me that Brian had opened a guarded channel of communication monitored by the figure of his lover. Her hair-do and essay on hand towels told me I was not to assume anything. Her advice to OUT OF LINE reminded me that I shouldn't mention what shouldn't be mentioned. So I took her advice to TO CALL OR NOT TO CALL. I answered casually, a short chatty letter, noticing lightly that his Christmas card was on the terse side. I was just opening his reply:

Dear Bob,
     I didn't write very much on my Christmas card because l) I'm in love with Jerry (truly) 2) I've got to start forgetting you (impossible) 3) It

didn't seem appropriate (why did I have to go to
Catholic school?). At any rate you will be happy
to know that in spite of my rude card I still think
of you quite often (in spite of myself).

Brian continued his parenthetical dialectic: I've
been watching a lot of B movies on the tube (one
of the times I think of you) and have decided
they're the best. (*Rock Around the World* with
Tommy Steele had me wearing a pompadour.)
(And they call Lourdes a miracle.)

Brian and I had coded our romance in camp
images; we craved these images, grateful that they
gave superficial expression to our deepest needs,
because the story of our community is the story of
doubt. We ironically befriended a past that had been
generally despised. Like our sex together, banality
took on a certain grandeur.

Brian and I made sex from family life, its
shattering rage that dwarfs Tragedy's pale accommo-
dations. We inhale rage, tedious as air; rage that not
merely dominates and bullies us like the binding
authority of a sacred book, but *is* us and consequently
lacks expression until I become Brian's father and
make Brian suck me off and then I piss on him while
he kneels, that first spurt of urine an outburst of
contentment that truly can be called domestic. Instead
of shattering rage what if I wrote shattering love—see
what I'm driving at? Banality may be the welcome
minus after a hot explosion of meaning. But we don't

need a month in the country to recoup from a little
water sports. I'm putting too big a name on—
simply—our love of structure. Structure takes pre-
cedence in banality, content is flattened. We make it
bear a new content, one that includes what the original
lacked; that is, we inform these flattened images with
our attraction for each other. They don't resist this
infusion of sexuality, they welcome it.

But I haven't mentioned the spirit of revenge
that motivates love for the banal: Scorching afternoons
after school, stranded in shopping center parking lots,
we ate pepperoni in the oily heat while the air above
miles of asphalt simmered and reduced like an existential French sauce. Desert hills and knolls and canyons
and scrub oak surrounded us but we lacked a language
to include them in our lives. 'Look,' we said, pointing
to distant peaks brought close by the focus of pure
desert air—we gazed at them through car windows,
our lips slightly parted. But even this description
colludes with a lying nostalgia. During my whole
childhood I was exhausted. Lack of meaning is
exhausting. I never realized that these neighborhoods
and childhoods were the eye of the tornado that the
U.S.A. is to the twentieth century. L.A. was so
undifferentiated that movement seemed inadequate,
remote: setting out on a walk like they do in books,
returning diminished and helpless, *miles* of tract hous-
ing defeating us at every turn: at the vanishing point a
couple of treeless kids in bathing suits would double
and shift like flames. Later, a hundred thousand

electric garage doors opened to receive the unwelcome fathers. Brian and I assuaged this memory of suffering by embracing it—the embrace conferring a human scale the original lacked. Then we offered ourselves— in the spirit of revenge—as myths produced by a dead society.

Brian closed with, 'Say hi to Lily, Bob, and take care of yourself and I beg you to forgive your bad boy for his rudeness.'

The first paragraph made me happy; the last discharged a shock that hit my nipples and groin. Dear Abby, is it wrong for me to meddle in his life? She replies: I used to have an answer to that question; now I don't.

I wrote back to Brian topic for topic, keeping a neutral tone. I described the pleasant delirium of watching sunlight fall mystically on white painted wood while listening to Mac, the 'mayor' of my street, give me a blow by blow account of his trip to the Serramonte Shopping Center to get his wheels aligned. I wrote about *Charlie's Angels*. When Farrah Fawcett kills someone and he explodes or plunges or slumps over his last breath as though in thought, she bites her lower lip and makes a vertical furrow named Remorse appear on her brow above the bridge of her nose to indicate the far side of emotional turmoil. I think her obviousness fascinated me, as though grief and despair were just another nostalgic set of codes to manipulate, abbreviate, like visiting Remorse Land at Disney World. I mentioned watching *Lassie* with Lily one day, when that compassionate dog saved another dog's life. A terrier had been caught in a nitroglycerin blast used to suffocate an out-of-control fire in an oil rig, and Lassie agreed to donate an emergency blood transfusion.

I closed with, 'You've been a rude boy. You know you have. Bad boy, you must know that I'm going to punish you. I have to punish you before I can forgive you—you realize that, don't you Brian?' I got a hardon as I wrote it. John Preston sent Jason, his slave, an envelope containing a few long steel pins. No words. I hardly aspire to that fierce poetry; it takes my breath away. Steel pins, Dear Abby? 'If Jason wants them, certainly, but has he thought about seeing his priest or rabbi? They wave good-bye from a sepia photograph. God bless and let me hear from you again. I care.'

Imagine Brian reading my letter: He's standing by his mailbox on the porch. It's impossible to depict for you all the voluptuousness of his figure. His eyes, his eyelids are heavy with it . . . He is intoxicated; he is no longer there; he no longer knows what he is doing. The left arm that he no longer has the strength to support comes to fall on a majolica flower pot, crushing the ice plant; the letter slips from his hand; the tips of his fingers rest on a window sill which has given them their position. See how indolently bent they are; he goes weak in the knees and a surge of joy carries him up. He lights a menthol cigarette and draws on it—I can taste it—he leans

The right arm that he no longer has the strength to support comes to fall
on a majolica flower pot, crushing the ice plant; the letter slips from his hand;
the tips of his fingers rest on a window sill which has given them their position
(p. 92).

After Jean-Baptiste Greuze,

Une jeune fille qui envoie un baiser par le fenêtre, appuyée sur les fleurs, qu'elle brise.

Engraved by Augustin de Saint-Aubin.

There's Bob gazing at his hard cock with the irresistible lust (yearning) of Ulysses being lured by the Sirens (p. 115).

Photo by David. Photo of Tom Rucker reprinted from *The Hot Male Review* with the permission of The Magazine Corporation of America.

back against the cool stucco wall—a line from a 50's song surfaces—'thrill my soul.' Masturbation occurs to him but before he can get his cock out he comes. There are only a few faint signs: a line of teeth appears below his lip, his breath catches and his eyes grow abstract. 'Bad boy,' he thinks, 'you made a mess. Shouldn't a done it—shouldn't a done it—I'm gonna tell on you.'

Joe-Toe/a close reading

THE BILL FOR two capuccinos at the Café Babar is $2.50 plus 16¢ tax. The cafe is jangly and feverish. As per usual, Jack announces brightly that he brought no money, just change, so he hopes I have some. For three seconds I grieve that Jack is poor, or is he? I take the bill and suggest he leave some tip but he protests that he needs coins for the bus. 'Jack, we're not taking the bus.' As I set two quarters next to my cup, he replies, 'Don't worry about it, Bob.' Spoken like a rich person. I don't know how to object without being a jerk so I shove my complaint to the back burner which is already crowded and getting hot.

Someone keeps staring at me so I wait outside while Jack talks to friends at other tables. It's a steamy night; I watch Jack through the glass: He presents himself, hands open. They tip their heads back while he smiles down, helping them along with engaging gestures and phrases and sometimes a bear hug: he projects extreme good will. It's exhausting. His face is red. Sweat drops from his curls and he mops his streaming forehead with a damp sleeve. That wetness trembles on the brink of sex, the disappearing funnel water makes as it empties down the drain.

WE WALKED TO his apartment. Car hoods reflected the chemical blaze of streetlights with a glare so artificial it seemed to ring; above, fast clouds—zigzags and dashes—showed gray against the stately blue-black. By one or two the wind that pushed those clouds would cool us but at ten we gazed up from a temporarily breathless heat. The moon rose full but undistinguished. We pointed out the sights to each other. Sensations seemed to stand out from their experiences like too much makeup. I directed Jack's attention to the ass of the man walking ahead, sheathed in thin-wale beige corduroy and alternately backlit and spotlighted by streetlights as we moved along. The ass arranged and rearranged the fabric like an expert; it circled and circled back, polishing a sexual core.

BOB: That man knows how to wear his ass. When I see an ass like that, I want to make this noise: uh!—an empty syllable I'd like to fill with my body.
JACK: He's really stacked.

BOB: Do you think he works out or is that genetic?
(Bob proposed that ass to Jack as though it constituted some rock bottom court of last resort.)
BOB: Are you angry about my trip to the baths?
JACK: It put a strain on our relationship.
BOB: Not sleeping with me puts a strain.
JACK: Why didn't you *tell me* you wanted to have sex? You know I love you very much.
BOB: You love me?
JACK: Yes I do.
BOB: *You love me?*
(Bob grew angrier and angrier. He considered rising into the heat as a corkscrew. They stopped talking. On Jack's corner they passed the laundromat with its smell of hot cotton; they arrived at Jack's and sat prim and forsaken on the edge of the bed surrounded by the heavy mood of his books with their odor of chocolate. Jack's hot skin was cold when Bob touched it; Bob was intolerably aroused and rejected by Jack's drenched curls and heat-spooked eyes.)
BOB (thought *fuck this* but bleated): Then why don't we ever have an intimate conversation?

I asked that question in all flats and abrasives, the song of the badly loved. By way of response Jack went from quiet to meditative while I mentally threw up my hands. Suspended as though in a thought balloon above his head, the faces of his friends agreed with him forever, flanked by little banners of wisdom scribed by Jack. He often asked me for a photo. I never replied but my silence stood for towering indignation—he hadn't exerted himself enough to possess me; no way was I going to end up as a smiling head tacked to a bulletin board. I sat forward; my anger was like riding in a speeding car. Jack got up and rummaged through the file drawer marked T and returned with a story. He said, 'I try to make my way toward wherever it is I'm not, in the company of whomever happens to be absent.' Jack had printed *Joe-Toe* in black in his fine hand, then typed the story on onion skin.

I applied myself like a Talmudic scholar decoding Jack the Unspoken, establishing principles and guides. The most foreboding aspect of the story was its total lack of pain: not in their coming together, not in their separation. That looked bad to me. I read it from Joe-Toe's point of view, contestatory, against Jack. Like Joe-Toe, I looked for a pang that marked the end of their affair. Alienation had become so refined it amused itself. I was dazzled.

It's not as though Jack were oblivious. His message to me through *Joe-Toe* was clear enough: 'Using language is for me a very public means of expression, like graffiti. I realize that I don't know how to use language intimately in a direct way . . . I know I had trouble being intimate even before I learned to associate intimacy with pain and self-humiliation. It's hard for me to tell one person what I wouldn't be able to tell twenty people or ten or five or ten thousand. I suspect that I want to be committed to Joe-Toe while seeming committed to no one. I want Joe-Toe to believe in my commitment to him while the rest of the world doesn't suspect it.'

That's it in black and white. I look up—Jack waves from the other side of the room: hello? good-bye? I should break for the door. What caused this highest form of oppression—the inability to take himself seriously? Is shame contagious? A panicky urge to 'save myself.' My characters are played by little squeaky voices, long rodent tails and not much depth . . . Triviality is a desperate condition: how do I show that events happen to these mice, destinies exist?

Jack, I am going to lose you and myself and our future, a portion of that loss already forms part of my present. I'm sunk. That's clear. I bridle against your assumptions about language—'the inanities,' you write, 'collecting toward orgasm.' That's by the Jack in us who circles wisdom passages in books and saves them like a greedy bank account. I'm rejected as a lover and a speaker. What about ordinary talk?—with Jack I aspire to the ordinary. What about orgasms? Playfulness is the site of our story, is that disowned too?

In a few paragraphs on lovemaking, Joe-Toe recedes into his own history which attracts Jack more than flesh and blood; Jack created Joe-Toe, the blond curls, the head cocked to the left as he walks, the smooth skin between his thighs, and now Jack dismantles him. Joe-Toe assumes his past—is banished into it—becoming younger and younger in his Catholic years (eighteen years old, thirteen years old, three years old and shouting to his elderly neighbor, male, 'Hello, my darling!') until he's a baby 'newly born . . . One of those wizened babes who spook the walls of the Uffizi . . . He howls in urgent infancy.' I'm in no position to criticize dismantling the beloved: it fortifies me as I shrink and he grows giant. *Jack tickles my chin with a Sequoia.* But Jack isn't afraid, so why deprive Joe-Toe of speech? Because: I am only a baby, when I hit I say I have been hit, when another baby falls I begin to cry; I identify slave with despot, actor with spectator, victim with seducer. Daddy will be my point of view and my symbolic order. How apt is this parent/child scheme as a model for tenderness? Isn't it Brian's? Perhaps each more deeply rendered sexual version of father and son gives Brian a further improved child-hood. Perhaps breaking that taboo is the fittest symbol of reconciliation. Perhaps all tenderness echoes this, the little appealing to the big. Beauty descends from a terrible height. Our moment of orgasm—poof! and myself the baby eagerly disappears—the opposite of divine conception, also seeded by the father's word.

But it's not love's meaning that confounds Jack—it's love's stupidity. From Jack's distance love is simple as water. Doesn't a person of minute distinc-tions crave less plebian fare? So he elevates love-making with verities. What is he doing to me? I wish he'd shut up and concentrate. Jack doesn't and the sex concludes with a perception rather than an orgasm.

I'm certainly in trouble, I think, lying on Jack's beige chenille bedspread. I keep thinking, I can't *do* this, I can't *do* this—what can't I do? Joe-Toe is growing more mysterious by the page. People are praying to him. But if Joe-Toe is a source, it's merely for puns, endless verbal substitutions: Joe-Toe—Ptolemy—Torii—Tourniquet—Torquemada—Turbot. Joe-Toe—Tonet—Tonal—Toenail—Tonality—Ptomaine—Tone Deaf—Tofu. Joe-Toe—Taupe—Torpor—Torah—Tort—Torsion. As a stream of words, he flows through Jack—Jack need do nothing at all to feel Joe-Toe empowering him forever. Joe-Toe becomes a religious principle, exiled from his own flesh. Jack need do nothing. Is this a compliment to Joe-Toe? I wonder where he is? Finally, in the last lines of the story I hear his voice, 'I needed to take myself far away from your glow so that I wouldn't touch it. I wanted to touch it so badly.' Longing, separation, darkness. Joe-Toe considers Jack: 'From the hill, from there above, I couldn't distract you from your glow.' What did Joe-Toe really say—at what cost—that Jack diminishes, tepid and artistic, floral as Ophelia's grievance? I try a sloppy 'Fuck you, Jack' but it sounds like a sloppier 'Don't hurt me' which brings me to the first lines of Jack's story, 'I'll tell you the ending in advance . . . He went off three days ago to New York, which to an actor equals breathing.'

Joe-Toe was not so much a story as a debate for and against story itself with Joe-Toe on the losing side. Jack, you are a fool a fool a fool a fool a fool to treat Joe-Toe as if he were a play on words or a perception or a motif.

Envoi

LADIES AND GENTLEMEN of the Future,

Greetings from late capitalism where meaning and image have come apart. I raise my hand in salutation or warning or good-bye—or muscle spasm? Is there going to be a future? Tell me. Yesteryears dressed in yesterday's fashions lean out from the balustrade of the sky. Their faces are elastic with comprehension, absorbed in a floating crap game; lips part; clouds opalate. Or are these years enclaves of timelessness: then reach up and take one down from the top shelf like a dusty can of peaches and taste the sweetness and silence that has always been gathering there. If there is no history, *fine*, if there is history, *fine*; if that's a mixed message, well, it fits the times. Our lives resist being turned into art and even though

I know (hope) you won't believe this, my fame would shine and I could make more money doing cut-ups so minimal our ears double their strength, or lists of silences brought to a peak of consciousness. That's why I'm writing to you—would you prefer silences to a morbid love story held together by a long freight train of equal signs and propelled by a modern emotion? I don't think there's a name for it yet; call it excited neutrality. You feel it in the space between image and meaning: an invented place but isn't heaven?—the future? Instead of cut-up phrases my characters are cut-up fryers from the supermarket dressed as engineers and passengers. I prod them onward hoping we don't all collapse into parts. What is self or narration without a future: my palms open with helplessness.

102

When you read this I will be ashes one way or another. The thought makes me wistful, confidential; can I be nostalgic for the future? Thinking to improve my diet and live long (salt, schmaltz) I asked my mom what our blood relations mainly died of. She replied *Fascism*. Concentration camps were never mentioned during my childhood. When I was eleven I learned about them from TV. I felt sordid and humiliated to be associated with so much suffering, and in public! Later I watch *The Sound of Music* on TV with my family. At the end the Von Trapps climb every mountain across the religious Alps to Switzerland—the plot continues in our movie: the musical nuns are murdered in their convent for shielding the

Von Trapps. The music is less lilting as the handsome young Nazi (he's just mixed up) shoots the silvery housekeeper in a ditch and also Max for his complicity and race. The Von Trapps' superficial decency gives way, the bottom falls out of our civilization as they sing a reprise of 'These Are a Few of my Favorite Things' to perk themselves up when they get wind of the Holocaust. That's what my family thinks when we watch the *The Sound of Music*. But—here I mentally slap my forehead—now I understand my parents' protectiveness. I had dismissed their anxiety as a droll ethnic stereotype. It's time for some direct questions—my mother tells me about the lives of relatives who were murdered by the Nazis. We have so many tokens of peace and comfort yet each life is marred by **103** violence. Do you get many letters like this, Dear Abbys of Things to Come? Violence is the rule. Believing in a future would mean so much to Jack and me in our lovemaking, and to my friends and the writers in my workshop, you have no idea. At worst it would make Jack's reserve easier to bear, not to mention the melting ice-cap, the ruined ozone layer, nuclear proliferation, the polluted oceans and the corresponding rallies and marches. First we stopped having grandparents and extended families so each life came to equal its biological span. It's really the end of religion and I'm less disturbed by the implication than by all the mess to clean up. Now the race numbers its own days so again we are thrown back on ourselves: Dread Prospect. I wonder if any of your other correspondents have the same problems. Just send an 8×10 glossy—write 'for Bob, Phyllis, Jack, Bruce, Denise, Joe-Toe and the Saturday afternoon workshop—'

Love,
Bob

A week passes: unable to reach Jack: tears, unanswered calls

WHILE JACK WAS good to look at, he didn't touch my first lovers—those two made statements with their bodies about the possibilities of physical beauty, statements italicized by their rapt sexual absorption. It still fills me with pain and pleasure to remember the lattice of muscle shifting a skin of satin with the least turn of Andy's head, and he really had a Tower of Lebanon. Or Ed—a Japanese mouth that looked like purple prose, that did resemble a rosebud filled with snow. Jack was disorienting; despite his meager sexuality he was hot; I wanted him in me. I wanted him to augment, I wanted him in my life and in my body so that I could exceed myself. At first I called this our private chemistry but now I see that augmenting is Jack's quality. His other friends recognize that. I imagine Joe also saw him as the stairway to a Joe-Toe known only briefly but liked on the spot. Their conversation interpreted two dancers extending every verbal gesture so that Joe-Toe was always being guided into a transforming lift. Still, Jack kept himself at a distance and stayed the same. If he's a medium it's water, light bends while Jack does not reorganize himself by a drop. He's lying down, alone. Even his own daydreaming self does not intrude. His features swim out, expand. He wonders, 'Am I sad?'—then realizes it's not a whisper of sadness running through his body but the noise of a distant plane. He always arrives from a far place where he keeps himself intact, departing from there reluctantly as a cat or ghost.

106 Joe-Toe had plenty of himself to spare so he gave lots away; no, for Joe-Toe to be himself he must give plenty away; he had enough to get up in the morning, to crack two eggs against the rim of a glass bowl, to be interested, to suffer, to waste. He admired people who broke down or fled—any honest response.

When I told my friend Sally about Jack she gasped with horror. She knew Jack; she'd met him a year ago and invited him to a dinner party. 'Jack arrived hours late, he brought someone—they marched from the front door to the buffet, ate like *pigs* and left.' Sally's anger was still so hot I wondered if she had been attracted to Jack. I asked, 'Was it a blond man? an actor?' No, it was a woman. I felt let down.

Jack fucked me hard as though Joe-Toe were watching. I became aware that each time he pushed into me I made a noise as though I were lifting something heavy—ugh! It sounded theatrical. When I grew silent he slowed down. Finally he asked, 'Are you all right?' Slower was better. My pleasure was metered out by the slap of his balls against my inner thighs, a coy, almost feathery touch, strange considering the enormity of the image. At a certain point I gave over and simply I was on a pole enjoying the sensation of intense meaning with no object to fix it on. I showed my gratitude by licking the pillow. Finally Jack climbed a series of quick intaken breaths. My orgasm was also 'high,' as though instead of propping myself on my knees with my face pushed into a pillow I stood on tiptoe emitting a high C.

Our heads rested side by side where they **107** had more or less stopped rolling. Our faces were so close that Jack's eye—almost touching mine—lost individuality. It looked like a medical chart: cornea, iris, lens. I slid a few inches away in order to recover him; I asked for a story from his childhood.

Jack turned to me in a voice filtered through a foreign drift of veils, 'Mein bed vass a sleigh from Pomerania und I haf yet the qvilt, how zen to ever part wis zis?—zis *touched* me vile I vust sleepink!'

'Jack?'

'Blumchen! Zee Despair ist sittink—how to schpeak zis?—down in my face! Vat a migraine! Vat a gnashink of mein teeth!'

'But Meine Kleine Nacht Musik,' I reasoned, 'if only mein Kuchen vould shtay forever bei me, und *cook* und *clean* und *vash* und be ein *slave* just ass am I to mein art!'

Jack kneaded my shoulders unconsciously; his eyes were exploded fuses, tantrums of perverse ecstasy, 'Ach ya! Ve could zuffer! und zuffer! und zuffer! und zuffer!'

I lay back and considered Jack. He sat up and returned my gaze with an affable smile. He traced the corolla of my right nipple saying, 'A pristine lily pad on a pool of rare hairy alabaster.' Then he traced the other saying, 'Look, Lily Pad East.' He gave me a kiss, then peered into my mouth.

'Plato's Cave?' I asked. He closed my lips and fluted them like a pie crust. I thought that was all, I was about to go to the toilet when he spread my legs apart and pushed his forefinger into my asshole where his sperm was; it made me gasp.

'Plato's Cave,' he replied. He exerted internal pressures against my taut bladder and involuted membranes. I wondered if he wanted me to roll over, to slap my ass maybe, but I felt it might be taken as a demand and I didn't want to discourage Jack in his desire to expose and dominate me. Let him put his hand in me as casually as in his pocket. I played with myself. Stroking a cock after orgasm yields pleasure in a class by itself—pleasure removed from any goal, so pure it's close to pain, Keatsian. Deglazing a pan, my mom says, 'It's a shame to waste a flavor.' I was not embarrassed to be so exposed; men have complimented my asshole, its placement and the elegance of its setting. Going one direction there's my perineum, pink ribbon, then the gladiola of my cock and balls. I toyed with them like a kid about to offer a bouquet. I was not embarrassed but if I were my shame also would have been a flower. In the other direction certain men discover an opposite inward turn where the two halves of my body fold into themselves, the reverse of a fountain. Or perhaps his finger was the stem and my body a flower—it's like sex for metaphors to be mixed (part wolf, part man, part bat, part cat). My cock wanted to carry my body up to Jack's mouth while my ass obeyed an opposite tropism, the urge to plant itself deeper on his finger which rotated monumentally. My whole body organized itself around it; my whole body and the full extent of my consciousness registered a nick of jagged nail. Right then I could have said, I love you. This sex, free of the libido's narrative demand for a climax, seemed more interesting to Jack. He searched for my prostate and wore a far away expression which I imagine I shared, brows furrowed, eyes on the distance.

A close reading: I can feel hunger in Jack by a moony tempo in him, lips slightly pulled back, an attentive expression. When Jack is tired he shows white around the irises and his sentences drop at the end. A certain vividness in his face and friskier body language mean he's about to shit: I extrapolate a small excitement in his elbows and knees, his saliva thickening. The back of his right hand—a fine web of wrinkle—then, mostly in the cracks, a scatter of

109

pinpoints that catch the light: he's sweating. When I say something banal or irritating his insides revolve and his irises slowly float away horizontally, banishing me to the outskirts. He always brushes his teeth for a long while because his gums want the abrasion—it makes me jealous.

BOB: Why did you lie about your age?

JACK: Why not? I couldn't assume we would ever meet again. I created that secret for the pleasure of revelation to heighten an intimate moment but then you looked through my wallet and spoiled it.

BOB (fixes Jack with a look. Then, hopelessly): There's a light comedy mood we should shake off.

Joe-Toe comes to fear this dreadful cheerfulness—the eyes of the Living Dead snap open, 'Have a nice day.'

BOB: We're so edited. What if I tell you something serious?

JACK: You have gonorrhea!

Heaven help the man in whose lover his safety resides. I imagine a Byronesque head in my lap, spit curls and Roman nose, whose future resides in me. He slowly opens his huge tormented eyes and murmurs, 'Dread Prospect.'

Dashing up stone steps a Scythian—his gold armor more interesting than what it contains—meets a Greek half naked for battle whose beauty is a physical assault. I the Scythian kneel, I surrender my sword on the flat of my palms and murmur *beautiful* in my language. I don't see but feel his cool sweep

sever my head and as it/I topples and rolls I hope to
catch one last glimpse of him before my senses die.

Jack smoothed my apprehension into a
pillow and punched a comfortable place for his head
to fall asleep on. He closed the chapter with an
allegory addressed to the globe of light suspended
from its brass chain, affording me only his small
profile:

Mr. Rappaport, an anthropologist, went to
Africa on a research project involving social forms and
bonding in gorilla society. It was an extended study
of animal behavior and he was stationed at a wildlife
compound for a number of years. During that time
Mr. Rappaport got to know the gorillas, became
friendly with them, but just before he was supposed
to return to the States one of them carried him off
into the jungle. The first search party gave up in a
week. It took the next one three weeks to find him.
He was flown, very hush-hush, to the States and
treated for shock and exposure, all very quietly.
Finally he regained enough strength to hold a press
conference and tell the world what he had been
through. Mr. Rappaport entered the room, very tense,
very nervous. The first question was, 'How do you
feel now?' He blurted out, 'How do you *think* I feel?
How would *you* feel? He *never* writes me, he *doesn't*
call . . .'

MUSIC BURST FROM the alarm clock: *Oh Jesus*!
With my eyes closed I asked Jack why he set the

alarm for gospel music. He said it wasn't. 'Then why are they singing about Jesus?' He said they weren't. I asked him again and he laughed, 'Bob, you're the one who said *Oh Jesus!*' 'Me?' I replied, astonished. 'I'm asleep, why would I sing gospel music?' I bore down into a heavy slumber and Jack went to shower.

I was dreaming that Phyllis's mother is a huge middle-aged bald man wearing a white duck shift. The three of us are standing on a knoll in the bright sunlight of a witty (brittle) literary conversation when Jack whispered, 'Time to get up.'

I answered with my eyes closed, 'Time to get up—an idea whose time has come.'

He whispered, '—whose time has passed.'

'An ancient concept.'

'Very old. The Greeks had a word for it.'

Sleep registered as a deep buzz. It took me a moment to name the warm and cool wing of air on my cheek. Jack must be kissing good-bye the one he loved. But my sleep proved stronger than his waking; he got in bed, draped an arm over my chest and dozed off. I smiled with my eyes closed, a smile I considered all day. I hadn't thought I was capable of a smile like that. It rose out of the center of my body from childhood; it expressed a bliss monitored by enormous hands, half as big as my being, the scent of Jergens and talk: I was mostly just a pulse and the sustaining hands were the prototype for familiarity, for cool smooth sheets to fall asleep in.

When I woke up Jack was gone—gone Saturday, Sunday, Monday, the next week, July . . .

Saint Venus

LACKING ITS PRIVATE story, I continue our affair single-handed in public images—sex the genre and my skin. Jack and I become imaginary; I'm brought to the boiling point and left to boil steadily away.

Not Delivered, Not Written,
Dear Jack,

Everything we do is nothing short of life itself.

There's Bob in soldier's helmet, his regulation T-shirt torn to tatters, his cock sticking up to his canvas equipment belt.

There's Bob, still belted, but now wearing coolly mirrored shades, beating off,

then tied to a pole and thrusting his hardon invitingly

forward as he struggles against the ties that bind. Like in any structure there's repetition but here—have you noticed—it's almost pornographic.

There's Bob in jock strap and torn white tank top, exhibitionistically displaying his erection and balls.

In the dream when I piss it must be masturbation because when I really piss too much it masturbates me. In the dream when he pisses it must be masturbation because when he really pisses too much it masturbates me.

Sitting in a doorway, his cock standing upright, aiming rigidly at his face.

There's Bob lying face down in the dirt, cock and balls jutting back between his legs. His hands spread his cheeks. We owe a debt of gratitude to the gay movement that now tough dudes take it up the ass as part of their charisma and manly charm. You laugh at this position? Bob knows what he wants—are you the one to fulfill his desire?

Choke him if he can't take a fuck.
Fuck him if he can't take a joke.

There's Bob in tight white T-shirt, his pecs and biceps bulging, his hands cradling his cock and balls.

There's Bob gazing at his hard cock with the irresistible lust (yearning) of Ulysses being lured by the Sirens.

115

There's Bob in a swimsuit; he doesn't notice that his cock and balls hang out, distended.

Bob huddles in bed with you as long as he can, in a state of surplus meaning. At 17 and a junior in high school, Bob's an average student and I guess you could call him an average guy.

Slowly increase the speed. Touch the skin more firmly as it becomes wetter dart press your fingers down on Bob's clit faster put your fingers together, thrust them into Bob two fingers right above the edge of the opening; Bob feels your fingers move into his belly, press against the muscle walls of his clit again.

There's Bob as he endures every sexual and torturous depravity known in his Olympian quest for the loincloth of the king of the Manazans. *Caligula* is a garden party compared to this heavy sex adventure.

There's Bob pulling away and sliding to his knees, turning you loosely into the spray of water, rinsing the soap away from your erect staff.

Wearing only white boxer shorts, Bob walks over and stands directly behind you, rubbing his groin into your scrubby jeans and wrapping his arms around your slender naked torso. In sex as in life, father to son,

man to man, buddy to buddy,

there's Bob: telephone jerk off calls, darkly lit sex clubs, circle jerks, movie houses—

116

Action: A prison fantasy that covers gang rapes, forced blow jobs and just a little bondage for color.

Under the threat of blackmail, you fucked Bob's face whenever you wanted. Some of the brothers asked Bob where he got his bruises. He told them playing football.

There's no character development. A tree can't exist in outer space, or fish in the fields, or blood in stone. They must have an orgasm to represent something to you. You immediately pick out a guy and say, okay

Ideal. And so he must ejaculate to represent much more than a guy that was stoned-out and getting fifty dollars to be fucked. He beckons to you but the door is incandescent—allow yourself a relentless longing.

There's Bob trying to lick the drippings from your balls, but you slap him across the cheek with the mass of your softening pole and order him to get up.

Bob's fingers tremble as he lifts your cock from his glass. Bob inspects the smooth bulbous cockhead, wet with tequila, then inserts it into his hungry mouth.

Stroking your cock, towering over Bob, you repeat the words you so often hear spoken about yourself. 'You're one handsome man,' you whisper, lowering your body over Bob's.

Approach the street door, open it, close it, go upstairs as quietly as possible, and turn into the little corridor to the right. The first door to the left in this corridor is mine. I'm innocent. Open that door with this big key, go into the dressing room on the right, where you will find a little candle by the light of which you can easily undress yourself. Do you understand all that?

You spray Bob in the face, in the eyes and all over his hair and mustache, while the red-haired dude hoses down Bob's buns and sends a few spurts up his back, getting Bob's shirt and collar wet in back. Bob has as many arms and legs as a snowflake. (If you can read this without feeling anything, give up.)

(Authority is mysterious, it can be studied forever.) There's Bob, beating off while you blow him, and now the feeling of your dick in his mouth and you come all over his face make him pop off, a big hot wad,

more butch, more intense, then tied to a pole and thrusting his hardon invitingly forward as he struggles against the tight

spasms of pleasure cross Bob's face each time the bulbous his head disappears into the palm of your hand. Bob lying back

Jack, to be frank with you, I find that the more wicked of us is not myself. Nasty hypocrite . . . if I believed in my existence as I believe in yours.

There's Bob going wild with all the manhood being pumped into him.

People are always asking Bob what he's going to do with his future. 'How is he?' asks one of the guys watching. 'Pretty good,' you answer. And right then you pull your dong out of Bob's mouth and shoot hot sperm all over his face.

If you severed Bob's head from his body while his body was still plugged in you might lift the head up and it might see its body having a great time for once in its life.

There's Bob in hot solo action or perhaps you like erotic play with plenty of stroking fingers, great chewing and sucking scenes and glorious butt-pounding.

There's Bob, a very boring guy with no personality, a TV addict and space cadet—any suggestions?

There's Bob, totally without affectations; you like that in a man.

There's Bob whispers 'Sit on my face' guiding you to the right position.

There's Bob, his cock straining inside his boxer shorts, forcing the warm meat of his member against his thigh. A prolonged moan erupts from the depths of his throat.

Suddenly we are a mass of moaning muscles contorting, towering, slapped, fondling, lubricating, ravaged, surging, spurting, arching, lowering, feverish, muscular, unzipped, chewing, sucking, sweating, oozing, bulging, forcing, stroking, throbbing, straining.

Jack, our young folk have returned to their ancient gods: Greed, Danger, Sex, Electricity, Padded Shoulders, Sex, Domination, Anxiety,

A degraded piece of fuck-meat: his facial expressions all different: pensive, suggestive, determined, inviting, naive, unconcerned, contemplative—and each of these has the overshadowing sexiness highlighted by that full dark mustache and those dreamy eyes.

There's Bob, only two feet tall, dragging his cock, heaves it over his shoulder like the seven dwarves, call him Bashful, when he laughs he covers his mouth— tee hee hee.

There's Bob looking up at you, you are a mountaintop view of life and death—jockstrap—metal studs—

Who What Where When Beginning Middle & End

Your loving object,

Bob

A grievance

EXCITED AND LONELY. 'Denise,' I
say, 'what if my mom reads that I did watersports?' I
wept the last time I saw *Little Women* on TV, with
envy for those chaste blue and gray Civil War uni-
forms, republican forebearance. A few weeks ago
some drunk asshole fag-bashed my boyfriend and *bit
him in the neck*. 'Christopher Columbus!' (I write for
gay men the same as La Fontaine wrote for the court
of Louis XIV—) Respectability, does it tally with
your life, mine? (—to be *universally* admired.) My
fantasies lacked the actual touching that diffuses the
shock of sex; I was in solitary confinement, Jack. Still,
the last chapter was hot, lively; I like its disorder,
desire that streams to all points of the compass. Zest
for experience equals the ability to sustain contradic-
tions like Jack's absence and my desire. It's a turn-on,

it's thrilling—images of men—myself—reflecting each other into infinity, responding to desire and producing it. I'd like you to experience some of this work of literature on your skin if possible. To me these public images are photos from a dream.

Like a dream, sex has no surface—it's experienced inside out. It's hard to assign a direction to this thought, like a figure at night—slender—I can't hear his footsteps and I'm not sure if he's walking toward me or away—I'm gripped by an uncontrolled fear. My senses were in an uproar. My deepest eroticism occurred in Jack's absence, even my imagination couldn't break through his self-containment. My images were of myself; it was myself who became continuous, flexible. Our affair took the form of my erotic revery and my skin touching my skin. Jack had withdrawn from the course of events but not from their beauty. Jack and I had become imaginary; he brought me to the boiling point and left me to boil steadily away.

Jack and I didn't have a present but I figured we would compensate with a great future. Previously I focused past Jack into that future but when I flew to L.A. Jack and the present stood clearly in my sights. I stopped being handsome, grew listless and small. On the plane I watched a beautiful man, tall, with the big gray eyes of an antique doll and also the doll's porcelain skin. I looked and looked at him: he was carrying a bunch of salmon roses. When I debarked I saw another beautiful man waiting. I stuck around

122

and sure enough man 2 was waiting for man 1, the flowers and a big kiss were exchanged. I caught sight of them again in the parking structure. They climbed into a maroon Thunderbird and their red hot tail lights burned with sexuality and performance.

My dad, home from the business, walked into the center of the bedroom and I felt the blandness of children before their parents. I got up with an ugh! 'One of us is getting old,' I said, kissing him on the cheek he offered.

He replied eagerly, 'It's me,' and raised his finger:

My roving days are over
My candle flame is out
What used to be my sex appeal
Is now my water spout.

I thought of Jack. I figured the hands of the clock would undress Jack and me and put us to bed. Seize the Day, I said to Jack, Remember Death.

I called Jack; he said he had been in New York, then San Luis Obispo to attend the pre-trial for blockading the entrance of a nuclear power plant two years ago. My return flight landed at eleven and by noon I was sailing across San Francisco. I wanted our reunion to open us inside out; his door opened as though it were inside me but his tone of voice said we hadn't experienced a break. An observation to the contrary betrayed an obviousness that embarrassed him. Certainly he was glad to see me but he didn't want to make love because of a meeting later. He thanked me for giving him the opportunity to miss me, he said he loved me but he didn't like sex during the day and he couldn't cancel his meeting because he felt he was finally making headway with a black man who would most likely be there. My eyes were beautiful but he was afraid of catching a disease. He listed them while we drank coffee in his yellow kitchen, bacterial and viral. A banana that had turned black presided there, sickening the air with its lush breath. It took me a moment to say, 'I never even had a disease—' But he shoved his spoon handle through the weft of a straw placement, then tormented his cup with it, then dragged a hand through his hair, too antsy, too tired, too many excuses. He rubbed his chin, 'Bob, you said you wanted us to see other people.' I had never said anything of the kind.

124

       'Jack, I never said anything of the kind.' I wanted to be a spring and double in half backwards. But Jack already shifted from distance to distance. Jack, Jack, Jack, Jack, Jack, Jack, Jack, Jack, Jack, Jack Jack Jack Jack Jack Jack—more real until less so, like a word said over and over. Pursuit committed me like a bullet but as a target he was circles spreading outward; when I approached his parts flew off. I had projected integration, an impossible expense of energy. What could unify a person at such close quarters—love? hatred? I had made Jack coherent but elusive, my complex organizing principle had produced a complexity whose disjunctions were small enough to convey an impression of depth, of secrets;

suddenly Jack appeared merely disorganized, subnormal, ramshackle and jerry-built, and I was committed to *nonsense*.

How did he see me? I experimented. 'I know I'm being a pest.' My sentence fell like a pebble down a well. After waiting in vain for a splash, 'I must be boring you.' I asked this in a higher voice—my fear annoyed me. Jack maintained that the opposite was true. 'I really can't believe this, Jack, do you think I'm a fool?'

Jack put a finger to his temple and deliberated a moment, 'No, you're not a fool.' I was startled. He took the question seriously, had to consider the answer. Finally, still smiling, I was humiliated. I couldn't have felt more suddenly chilled and excluded if I'd learned Jack was a ghost. In that moment our affair had run its course, the rest was denouement. All that remained was to wait disconsolately for phone calls; to degrade my time by stitching and unstitching each message from the beyond, each cancelled date; to read his horoscope; to drive past his house mournfully, as full of urns as a Roman graveyard. On his chenille bedspread I began composing the sentence, 'If Jack and I didn't have much of a present I figured we would compensate with a great future.' (At that moment I lost my innocence: Jack didn't suspect he had become evidence for the prosecution—biased record, stacked jury.) Why not write a story about how people we love extend us and their loss is the door of our life slammed shut in our face? (A young man married a young woman named Yuki. That means snow. Yuki proved to be a loving wife and good mother. After some years the husband told Yuki that, sitting there with a white light on her face, she reminded him of an episode from his youth. During a blizzard he and an older man took refuge in a mountain hut. A snow spirit named Yuki-onna entered and breathed over the older man. She approached the younger and told him she would spare him if he promised never to mention her visit. The old man was dead in the morning.

Suddenly Yuki's human appearance and natural color changes and she sits revealed as the Snow Woman. Her husband just related the story of herself—intolerable to this divinity who exists above or below articulation. The story partializes her; for him it makes her actual. In quiet fury she reminds her husband of his promise never to mention her visit, and tells him if not for their children she'd kill him instantly. Instead she melts away without reorganizing herself by a drop. This man could not have felt more chilled and excluded. He sinks down, cross-legged on a tatami mat. Even as his shocked understanding grasps and releases again and again this wild event—even as he gazes at the puddle of pure water his wife has become, immortal remains of an immortal deity, soon to be a lake if he pours into it the tears he will shed—even as woe rocks his body back and forth, he questions himself:

'Well, I told it badly. Certainly there was

Her husband just related the story of herself – intolerable to this divinity who exists above or below articulation (p. 126).

It never lets up, Jack. It shapeshifts from an ordinary American citizen (p. 146).

An American Werewolf in London. Copyright © by Universal City Studios, Inc.

Courtesy of MCA Publishing Rights, a Division of MCA Inc.

some problem with the ordeal of the blizzard. I should have made more of the weather the night the old man died, modulated the tempo, added a metaphor or two—*the night was white as the blank page of*—and I didn't describe Yuki-onna—dressed in maple leaves though it was dead winter and bringing through the storm the absolute silence of a mirror, the silence of an object standing midair, completely out of context, alienating. I could only describe her figure by the break in space it created. Why not write a story about how the loss of my Yuki is the door of my life slammed shut in my face?' He concludes, 'Oh my Lord and my God, grant me the grace to produce a story which will prove to me that I am not the lowest of men, that I am not below those whom I despise.')

'Jack, I have a grievance.' I sat on the high stool. A cold nausea mounted from just beneath my diaphragm, my palms were sweaty, my throat tightened; my lips went dry and my breathing became irregular. I wondered if Joe-Toe felt this way or whether he abandoned his body when it no longer interested Jack. Did Joe-Toe feel the major symptoms? What about the fine tuning? Slight dizziness, sudden sensitivity in his erotic zones—the skin, unconvinced, yammers for a caress.

Jack was sprawled and diffused on the brown corduroy pillows beneath me. He furrowed his brow politely—at least he should have a little fear. Maybe he assumed I never really loved him. Maybe he was right. Maybe I wanted to acquire him, like a happy ending, like a refrigerator. Could a labor-saving device be my other? Maybe I mistook knowing the same things for knowing him. Still, how else do we know people; still, is that all it comes to? 'Jack, for the last four months I've tried. I give up. You're a fool Jack—you're not going to do any better than me.' It was unreal; disagreement had never existed verbally; I had no precedent for this conflict; I spoke through dead lips; I was null and void. Intense boredom and a sudden urge to sleep and dream robbed me of consequence.

Jack's face swims away and starts doing laps. He wants a relationship so pure it doesn't exist: heroic, creative, unique, original, abstract, elevating, 'interesting.' No intimacy, no trouble, no story. I want a relationship with historical precedent, societal messages, old gestures with new meanings; a relationship that's ordinary, inconsistent, 'boring,' physical: if there are any sensitive men who want some action, give me a call. So hot men in tight jeans, in jock straps, in flannel, in three-piece suits, in jogging outfits, in chaps, in leotards electrify my bed but we fuck intensely in order to assuage a longing larger than any particular person, a longing for happiness predicated on a beautiful turn of the head, good forearms, nice basket, nice ass, a dark Russian smile, a blond smile, a glower—longing based on distance; distance is compelling and these encounters are the erotics of distance. We page through each other's bodies like a porno magazine where after fifteen seconds you turn to maintain a buzz. I agreed to the terms and foundered in them. Jack was my totally evil enemy—I began to understand that. (Jack inquired, *Evil strange or evil ha ha?*) I wanted him to worship me, then I would take a small-minded revenge like invalidating his personality which I viewed as four or five bad habits. (Jack said, *The only friends we don't spare—who do not escape our scrutiny—are our lovers and those who become our enemies.*) I caught his attention and asked him to respond. He might have said, Why do you always make a mess? Instead he looked steadily into my eyes directly addressing the Bob in here, 'I love you the best. There's no one but you. You're beautiful. I love your writing.' He said it like the long awaited truth that conquers the world's falsehood.   **129** The high contour of his cheek and his glossy curls convinced me.

All right. I provided a sympathetic excuse, one with plenty of generality so that it would not bind us; we could jettison his previous conduct by giving it a name. I rested my hands on my gently spread knees like a therapist and said, 'I want to be close to you, are you afraid?' Jack flashed a worried grin and opened his palms, then proposed something about love, people and fear—we were surrounded by tens of thousands of book pages with ink lines circling similar thoughts. I thanked him for words to live by and pressed on.

'I have a grievance. I'm angry at you. You're a political man—aren't you obliged to be responsible for your actions? Your words?-I'm *angry* at you. What kind of future do we have? You say you love me. Then you invent a legion of alternatives to me which I'll refrain from listing: *first* you say you're too busy, *plus* you want a black man, *plus* Joe-Toe is arriving in two weeks and you have to concentrate on his arrival, *plus* you are never on time—in fact, you don't seem to know what time *is*, *plus* you'd rather be celibate, *plus* you want an affair with a woman and *finally* you equate me with the world's diseases.' My back was sore. How disheveled I felt, like before sleep at the end of a paragraph when I realize I understood all the phrases without stitching them into meaning.

130   Meaning. His withholding seemed selfish to me, as though emotion were a treasure horde. Can that be right (face screwed up)? Was my part better? I never said I loved him. There's no one scale that can arrange facts and assign value here. Neither of us dismissed his personality's standing army. Jack said he loved me; I was faintly repelled. A kernel of reluctance in me wants to refuse: my times, language, nature when it fiddles with my body, self—intolerable metronome. One object is a question (a bomb), two objects are a paradox (bigger bomb) so it's a relief when a magician makes them vanish in a blaze of crossed circuits or petty bureaucratic offenses or the imagination or my mother's body—nurturing pyra-mid in the sky that reduces me to a goo goo. How dare words name things—
DAY: as though you hang a blue window on the wall.

NIGHT: as though you dip two fingers in a bucket of indigo and hold them up.

I'm nothing and my creed is nothing. Matter is energy repressed into shape so it's *eager* to disappear, so *naturally* we want to be part of the explosion. Everything wants to die. The empty space takes my breath away.

But nihilism didn't make me uncomfortable. I started out from there; to remain would be cozy, lazy. My misfortune was that I lacked Jack's love; Jack's cock was the toothpick that stabilized my club sandwich of being and nothingness.

What really hurt was injured pride, an ordinary pain. Like a gyroscope the speeding orbits of my considering came down on that one point. Like any position it became uncomfortable. Who wanted Jack or Jack's cock or any cock—a turkey neck wearing a fireman's hat! History and self are narrative puzzles— what to reject or accept? We felt that nothing bad could happen, or the worst already happened, yet even a casual glance—Like Jack's *Joe-Toe* there *is* no story. Jack was never going to be, I was never intimate with—*I*—so I substituted intimacy as a weapon.

One tear falls from Jack's left eye, the closest to me, drawing a crooked path of reflected light over his cheek down to his jaw where whiskers detain it. I almost succumb—to what? I don't know why he's crying, why he doesn't wipe the tear away or if this tear is the product of years of drama training. I have a pang of regret—a wide avenue leading to other regrets. I glance down it but don't take it. The way to combat this tear is simply not to be moved.

My face became more and more set. I didn't speak: our silence was a tennis ball tossed high in the center of the room. When it stopped Jack cleared his voice and said, 'I had no idea you see me as irresponsible. I should ask my other friends. Maybe I should be alone for a year and think about these things—sort out what I want and my image of myself and the way people see me.' He would not harden into a position against me so I couldn't even compromise. He thanked me for sharing my point of view. He presented himself as a collaboration, a work in progress.

I said good-bye to the 'me' who lived through Jack. It was time to say it out loud. I had refrained out of cowardice but my position was intolerable; verbally I was nowhere. Speech would give shape and a tense to the bad news and signal the beginning of a mourning period. I tried to steady my breath.

BOB: Okay, let's settle it—then we won't be lovers. (That's the first time the word lover is spoken.)

JACK: Not necessarily.

(Bob is thunderstruck.)

BOB: Jack, do you think I'm going to give you a raincheck?

JACK: I want you in my life.

(It's what Bob said to Brian.)

I gathered myself to go. Jack pulled himself together and got to his feet; I ran an obstacle course of loving hugs and sincere pats of encouragement and said good-bye on the landing under the porch light with its waxy glass shade. He drew me into his embrace—my arms hung limp; finally I dared to touch the base of his spine where his ass begins. Jack said, 'You're beautiful.' What did he mean? Was that a consolation prize? I mentally filed it with his single tear. Still, wasn't I seduced?—into what?

Map of tender

134   DURING JULY PHYLLIS stayed with her other son in San Diego. In August she returned, and after the Saturday workshop we met for coffee in a café on 24th St. that I always disliked. The food wasn't bad, the coffee was good, so it must have been—as the classical music d.j.s say—the *ambiance*. I'll describe the place to you just to pause a moment before a difficult scene. They had remodeled; now it was upwardly mobile, a large dim room: white walls, blue molding and ceiling, blue and white plastic tablecloths that mimed a Jacquard check and lots of verathaned knotty-pine paneling. Before it had been hippyish with a dusty jungle of unhappy plants and loud music. The music remained, the sound system was still mostly backbeat and behind it a baby still cried in listless continuum. The new colors failed for

the same reason as the plants—no daylight rescued them from being inert chemicals, so the landscape mirrored my story's emotional devastation like the blasted oaks of Nineteenth-Century Lit. The food was good but sad; I imagined the meat retained some of the mechanical brutality that brought it to this pass. It was just the Acme—not Andy's where you could have fun, or Hopwell's where you could be happy.

Phyllis and I ordered capuccinos at the coffee bar, paid for our own and found a table where a small glass held purple amaranths (prince's feather? love-lies-bleeding?) Phyllis tasted hers, replaced the cup on its saucer and told the coffee it was delicious. It had a clean round flavor; cinnamon, rusty, flecked the dry beige foam mounded on the flat wet surface. We were both nostalgic about food and saw this coffee as a window on capuccinos of days gone by. Phyllis wore pants as usual, and a silk shirt, mauve, a tweed jacket and a silk scarf which may have alluded to coffee shops, writers and *la vie bohème*. Her butterscotch hair was parted and hung straight; she wore no makeup, a little lipstick.

I asked about Peter's death. She told me the story from beginning to end in clinical detail, his pulse, his blood pressure's decline and the diminishing of other vital signs—heart and respiration. Even the angle of the bullet. Perhaps she knew all this because there was so little story. She said, 'On Friday he went out for groceries in Oakland where he and Susan

135

lived. He went to the corner store and was apparently held up and shot for a roll of eight dollar bills Susan said he went out with. I only gradually understood that it was very serious. A sure strong black doctor who had been brought in to help the on-duty doctor talked to us. It became clear that Peter was ruined. Later, Susan told me the things he said. 'I've been shot in the leg.' She said he sounded rather astonished. 'No, Petey, you're shot in the chest.' The hole in his chest showed burn and was small. He said, 'It was a blank. It was a joke.'

'And then the last thing: 'I'm going into shock.' I know how he would have said it, probably mildly, with some surprise, with full recognition and knowledge in his voice of what was happening to himself and to others.'

Phyllis talked about Peter with such respect-ful affection that I found myself missing him. 'Was there a police inquiry?' She supposed so but it didn't interest her. She pushed an investigation away from her in the form of her coffee cup. The bureaucracy of crime and retribution was a Tower of Babel stunned to silence by the depth that follows a catastrophe. Phyllis touched a few freckles of cinnamon on her saucer, then laced her fingers together. She said, 'He was always *open* to what was going on emotionally, quick to the current. He had the extraordinary gener-osity to give people their due. I could talk to him—he would *be* there.' Phyllis's eyes gleamed, she bowed her head and folded her hands in her lap. She's so secure that she can sit with strangers and, if she's concentrating, close her eyes for a long time. I imaged her absorbed in mourning the part of herself called into being by Peter. She was no longer in the café. After a minute I realized that her chest was not rising or falling. An anxious smile shaped itself on my face and my eyes began to widen. Finally she raised her head and resumed breathing; her face was streaked with tears.

Then Phyllis cried, very frankly. Tears gathered and fell, gathered and fell. She didn't even bother to wipe them. She wasn't pitted against herself when she cried—no gasps or convulsions. She cried and apologized without sincerity for making a public display. She continued, 'Susan was a fine girlfriend. For years he had been with a woman who wasn't— she had a son from an earlier marriage and Peter put a lot into fathering him. I'm glad he had a glimpse of that. One day he told me he was bisexual and said he didn't understand why everyone shouldn't be.' Phyllis said one of his ex-boyfriends attended the funeral. I mentioned the blond man's 'We all loved him in our way' but Phyllis corrected me. That man had a daughter who almost died. I had taken a parent's emotion for a lover's.

She said that Peter's bisexuality was one reason my writing interested her, so she could better understand love between men. Her candor struck me as a pedigree. We were closer now than we had been during the two years of the workshop. She thought I hadn't liked her. I countered, 'You always deflected my attention. Besides, you write beautifully.'

Phyllis protested, 'Why should I *want* to be a writer? Why isolate myself? I could go to Europe this summer—maybe for the last time—although that's what I've said before every trip since I was fifty. Why stay home and write?'

'It beats me. If nine-tenths of the writers I know were going to quit, I'd say with Grace Paley's Aunt Rose, 'Good-bye and good luck.' But I have an impulse to colonize you. (Here we laughed.) Yes, colonize. Phyllis, you are an island, a very nice island, but wouldn't you be better with a little pineapple plantation—produce, produce!'

138

Phyllis flashed a big rectangular smile, chin up, as though she were sprayed with water on a tropical day. *'Pass the salt!'* she announced rather startlingly. It turned out to be instant slang for agreement. I enjoyed her voice, sweet/sour, able to italicize with drama, a vertical quality with all consonants pronounced. She was laughing now. I related a piece of gossip Ed, my ex, told me about his cousin Sonny and Sonny's mother, Aunt Dot. It was public knowledge in Ed's family that for forty-five years the mother and son, who were both obese, had slept together in the same single bed. The thought tickled me. I wondered if my story were daring but Phyllis laughed and said, 'How delicious, like two baked apples.'

I wanted reassurance that Phyllis would be

all right. I had no illusion about who was receiving solace. We returned to Peter, kept returning. In any case, we were close and it couldn't last so we filled the brief time with an urgent rush of confidences—our families, our mutual friends, our boyfriends—caffeine hurrying us up. Although I turned Jack and me into a joke, she paid me the compliment of taking us seriously. I had thought she was rich; referring to her sons in public, she used their nicknames. I learned her glamorous familiarity came from sharing a literary life with the husband she later divorced. I liked to imagine Phyllis as the hero of her own life. She looked out for herself and her current beau was no exception; he didn't make demands and kept himself small. Phyllis admired my pink sweatshirt and silver and lapis ring. 'Bob, you've had your colors done,' she laughed.

139

We discovered that we both loved delica-tessens and cafés so our conversation turned to French fries, chili, falafel, pizza, stuffed grape leaves to go, Dragon Burgers, baloney on white from food mobiles parked outside suburban office towers, fish burgers, Jim's superburgers, EAT. In downtowns and the suburbs I want to stop at every café and diner. It's the nearest I have to a religion. In Red's Java House I eat frosty blue twilight, the Big American Sadness. Doesn't nostalgia intrude between me and French dip? I pour nostalgia over crushed ice and drink it. I live in a country whose military budget is thirty-four million dollars an hour; I squeeze that fact out of a ketchup bottle. We noted distinctions and culinary shadings from melancholy to cynicism to abstraction. Red's serves old mortality but in McDonald's we eat the void.

I wanted to extrapolate from Phyllis to Peter. If he resembled her he must have been very fine. I imagined loving him, being his lover, waiting at a window of longing for him to arrive. I felt that by desiring him I was beginning to understand his death. Phyllis said, 'I found caches of his cigarette butts around the house, I hunted for them, and even though I don't smoke I smoked them all.' I had a shock of recognition. So, I thought, a parent's love for a child is not different from the love between lovers, not merely as intense but cut from the same cloth.

The last swallow of coffee contained the most sugar. I bade the amaranths a mental adieu. When we entered the Acme it was sunny. A salty 4:30 wind had come up, dark and bright. A pending rain gave everyone in the street a conspiratorial feeling that registered as tremulous sexuality. We opened our eyes wider, quickened our awareness. Phyllis and I walked down 24th to her bus stop at Dolores just as the bus swung over and folded its yellow doors. It came faster than we thought. I embraced Phyllis and kissed her on the mouth. The kiss surprised us. I think she held out her cheek. Drawing back, I looked at Phyllis's lips where my lips had been and then at her eyes. They were lowered, bashful or embarrassed, but later I realized that she was just looking at my mouth where her lips had been and if she had glanced up I also would have appeared bashful, eyes lowered. My kiss was for Peter as much as Phyllis. It struck me as important that we looked at each other's lips like mirrors although I can't say why. Maybe it was that our surprise showed in precisely the same gesture and for an instant we spilled into each other. Phyllis climbed into the bus which immediately lumbered away down 24th St.

A continuum of experience

142

dear bobby,

yesterday i blew off work because it was such a gorgeous day people in the street were saying hello and smiling and i wouldn't miss that for the world. however, wound up drunk, broke, and hustling drinks, fun, but a little sad, really just stayed on a little longer than i should have. some say that deep in my heart i'm a slob. well, i pray for the safety of their progeny tucked away in those tight kleins.

i got up with a hangover and a dream fresh in mind, you and i are walking the streets, you have been transformed into a little egg cup with bird legs, later you are yourself.

i thought maybe i'll go shopping, if i can't be good at making it today, i'll spend it today. today had one of those summer mornings san francisco is notorious for, cold and AAAGGGHHHHHHHH!!!!!! this is really our first dose of it this year, summer is peculiarly late this august. i keep seeing a guy at the stud, i like him a lot and he is pretty natural, makes me feel good, an italian. i introduced him to your jack. jack was dancing with a blond actor who looked like gay doom. as it turns out unsurprisingly they all knew each other from circles of friends that go back probably to my first shaving kit. my italian said something like, oh so that's jack. the wheels start turning and i say, will the real Mr. Show Business please sit down.

bobby, why is it whenever you see a demolition site it looks like the last 30 years of mainstream american art. coming to terms with your materials— **143** ha!

while waiting for the bus i notice a guy with a fashionable leather jacket and a hot ass, something is peculiar about him, he is observant and stalks around the bus stop, his head turning here and there, he's carrying a plastic bag and a gray lunch pail, he hasn't been socialized properly, he is rough looking . . . i keep an eye on him and when the bus arrives i sit down two seats behind him to observe, he turns his head slightly and there on his right cheek just below his eye is a tattooed tear, a custom of cons, this guy is an ex-con and i'm cruising him, more impending doom, you just put your quizzical little toe in the tarpit and a hundred thousand years later someone's peering at your femur and thinking nobel prize. i can't help to think that that ass of his caused him a lot of trouble in prison.

i get off at his stop and i am really curious bobby, i can't help it i followed him up to filbert steps and gave up, what would a hardcore, offbeat person have to do with tres chic filbert steps beats me.

so i wander north beach, looking in bookstores, the benign kind, feel the focus of attention at times, buy colored pencils and shrimp and take it home, home finally, home safe, put on an album and write to bobby.

even when you find
you've given all
and nothing's come back to you
just remember
keep your little chin up
till you find someone who's
loving you.
song lyrics.

keep your little chin up,
tommy

p.s.

there are 3 asparaguses trying to cross 101 during rush hour, they argue about who will cross first, finally the two convince the third to cross first, he steps out and sure enough a semi zooms by and flattens him, they call an ambulance and go to the hospital.

the two asparaguses are very upset, pacing the waiting room and saying, 'oh god, this is terrible!'

finally a doctor comes out and they say, 'doc, is he OK?' and the doctor says, 'i have some good news and some bad news, the good news is that your friend will live. the bad news is that he will be a vegetable for the rest of his life—'

Do you think Lazarus can warm his blue hands
by holding them up to the blue Northern
Lights?

146   (TO BE LOVED and not touched—it
made me feel abstract, like an idea. A wave of
nostalgia carried me away. I tried to remember when
water was wet, stone hard, sky blue. Jack's bent
elbow made me wistful for bending elbows.)
JACK: I don't want to catch a disease. The wages of
sin.
BOB: Is death. That scans well. What it forgets is
that the wages of *everything*—
JACK: You men are beasts.
BOB: When the moon is full and bright, Jack. It never
lets up, Jack. It shapeshifts from an ordinary American citizen. I'd shoot it off but I lost my silver bullet
and I'm afraid of hitting my foot. (I find the intensity
I longed for but I'm stuck at the metaphor's *is*—
without a future all forms present themselves but

without that future I can't become any of them. Jack
has withdrawn taking the world with him; the impossibility of being loved by him comes to equal the
impossibility of being loved by anyone—*and if it
became a vegetable for the rest of its life?* I am hysterical,
overwrought, bitter, overbearing, pinpoint, insulted,
I talk too much, I'm hopelessly overfocused, manipu-
lative, calculating, deferential and complex. Jack sticks
his fingers in his ears. I'm stumped. I can't account
for this huge foolish expense that doesn't buy meaning
or any consolation for being separated from my
mother. I can't get comfortable in bed: all my scars
start to itch and my tongue hurts. These refinements
of misery enchant you like the tales of Sinbad. Shallow sleep, tedious dreams: *Do you want a child? Yes,*   **147**
*yes, a son like Schnabel would paint: one outline on a field
of broken dishes . . . then we'd take off all our clothes . . .
and I'd go down on him. I see you love animals. Yes,
especially dogs, see, there's a dog over there. I* love *animals.
I* love *you. How degrading, degraded; pet, pet.* This will
break and I will be scattered. Just a little will so
confuse me that my spine will crawl down itself
and my muscles lose the fiction of ability. I forget
to write down a check number. Someone looks up
from a desk and says, 'Don't you ever *listen* to *anything*
I tell you?' Then what if other *everyday* distinctions
appear as remote as that number, so that I don't bathe
or wipe my ass—smells, the most regulated and
feared. I can't remember about farting corrosive
intersteller gasses, noises like a straw at the bottom of

a glass, or speaking too close to your face, the stench peeling your skin back, and certainly then I will be surrounded by voices coming from the inside and outside, whispering in my ear as though I'd said it— Why don't you ever *listen* to anything I *say*? I *told* you to stop *pissing* in your *bed*. Trill: It's time for us to take our bath now. Downshift to: Christ! You shit in your pants *again!* Or worse: Dear me Mr. Gluck, we shit in our pants again?) (Or better: return to childhood, never empty cup of remorse and boredom—a blue bandana emerges from Jack's pocket, he *wipes my nose*. Leaving his apartment, he slowly rotates his massive head, *Do you have to go to the bathroom?*) (On the other hand, I obeyed the imperatives of breakfast and dinner and work. I had a lot to do: writing workshops, flyers, the galleys for *Elements*, a pending visit from cousin Mike—*wash sheets on guest bed*. I needed friends; Denise gallantly took me under her wing. How often do I get the chance to be unhappy in a novel? Still, I don't want this story to be less complex. I would have dumped Jack, I was above him and he bored me. The drudgery of the whole scenario bored me. Jack wouldn't let me be a baby and minus that disintegrating magic only vanity and obsession remained. *Vanity?* That's not it. Nothing is it. *It* thrashes in the dungeon of relentless clichés. *Dungeon?* Nothing ever fit. My lovers were a melting pot but shared—except for Brian—a power based on with-holding. Jack was typical; he was not worst but last. He canceled my idea of the future. I struggled against and welcomed the catastrophe. We failed to push into history—we sailed a galleon under the flag of a Christian nation drearily toward the edge of the flat world. I kept shrugging mentally, 'This has nothing to do with me.') (A year later Jack wanted to be lovers in earnest and I said no thanks without pain or pleasure.)

JACK: We hardly get a chance to see each other, why spoil it? I don't want to sleep with everyone.

BOB: Not with the entire human race—I'm its local representative. Gather ye rosebuds, Jack. Carpe diem, Jack. Time and tide, Jack.

(Bob sat on Jack, straddling his chest. Bob shook Jack's shoulders. Jack laughed: *Cute Marches On, Bob.* He loved wisdom. Failing to locate a certain book in his library, he remembered with exasperation that it must be one of the volumes Joe-Toe carted out and threw away—in the spirit of self-preservation, Bob surmised. *Against the superiority of another person there is no other remedy but love.* Bob's assessment of Jack's charms acquired a hostility. My gorge rises as I picture Jack circling this passage. *Behavior is a mirror which reflects the image of everyone.*)

Once I rimmed him: he was balanced on the back of his neck, his ass straight up and I had my face in it. It smelled like the inside of a pumpkin. I pulled back and considered his Desert Pink hole with its nimbus of black curls that my saliva had matted into points circling the All or Nothing like Tibetan flames. His upside down face seemed simpleminded, surprisingly bland and slack—I wondered what he was thinking about. He noticed me and waved from a jaunty distance. *Good manners should enhance personality. We desire the unusual, but it should not be embarrassing.* At heart I'm a masochist yet I'm a coward—masochism is so pleasurable that I draw back. O God, I pray in totally bad faith, don't make me a masochist—already my knees are bending before whatever it is I love, the better to worship it. *No one is a greater slave than he who imagines himself free when he is not free.*

In lovemaking Jack's focus was not appealing. *The greatest human beings are always connected to their century by some weakness.* He detained me with winks, smiles, nicknames and friendly encouragement—always reminding me who I am. *In society we accept everyone as he appears to be, but he must appear to be something.* That's a freedom—to have sex and remain yourself. But there's a freedom at the opposite pole—to forget who you are. *Behavior is a mirror which reflects the image of everyone.* I already knew the former, the latter interested me more. *We desire the unusual. Behavior is a mirror.* I felt my desire to be merely a piece of meat was on the side of history, though that made the issue no more simple or complex.

Little Allegory

A knock: a convulsed yip from Lily—then she's on her feet barking loud at the door. There's no point disciplining her, this behavior reflects a Lily who has nothing to do with Bob. She dashes to her food bowl to make sure it's empty (she's not into sharing), then rounds up her bones: one from the bedroom, one from the kitchen. She positions herself in the hall, at once guarding the bones and displaying them. One remains in her mouth so she's unable to do more than growl whereas her whole rump wags in a flurry of urgent greeting (don't hurt me) and her tail is a white blur of unconditional surrender. Bob opens the door, says, 'And what are you?' One centimeter above their heads roars a harrowing wind but they stand in dead calm. Lechery pokes Bob in the ribs, 'I am one that loves an inch of raw mutton better than an ell of fried stockfish, and the first letter of my name begins with Lechery.' It pushes past Bob into the living room and sits down on the Queen Anne double-cane wingback with arms of black lacquer swarming with insects and lizards painted in gold. Jack replies, 'Listen to me, I'm speaking like a book: irritation that never gets soothed, wanting one more caress as a lifestyle, unless someone wants to fuck you l) you are lonely 2) not valuable 3) whining for sex like a junkyard dog.'

LECHERY: Sign of life, human contact, pleasure.

JACK: First you turn yellow followed by an itch or drip, a burning sensation, then a chancre, sores, warts—a small pain in your chest, corkscrews in your brain, purple dots and—

LUST: Alas! (appeals) You are able to see yourselves as sexual objects. Still, you're socialized as men: you see your bodies as a challenge, a Mount Everest, so you are sexual daredevils, explorers, mountain climbers.

BOB: I'd like to draw the line if I could find one—is water sports okay but fistfucking out? What about gerbils?

LECHERY (blanches). *Gerbils?*

A KNOCK AT the door: Lily's on her feet again: food bowl, bones, hall, but with less commitment to barking and wagging. Bob answers. Enter Pride-Personelle Proud-Heart bringing an odor of old varnish and toast. It makes itself comfortable on the walnut Regency sofa upholstered in beige linen velvet. Both Lechery and Pride are robed in the thousand folds of allegory. When time stops, life becomes opaque *as though* out the window instead of blue sky Bob sees the solid gold parquetry of heaven—filigreed cartouches house blue angels *as though* they are mounted sapphires with their hands raised *as though* conducting an orchestra. Jack also sits on the sofa, Bob's on the Stickley Bros. Mission Oak armchair, Lechery remains on the double-cane wingback and Lily dozes off beside the brass Deco torchier; she's on her side, legs extended, head tilted back like a flying Pegasus.

BOB (says to Pride-Personelle): You *brag* about being an emotional cripple.

PRIDE (stands up affronted): Analysis implies distance! Sense of proportion! Self-respect! Double chaste against all suit! Fighting to win! I am discontinuous and I love taboos!

LUST: *I* love taboos! Sit down, Vanilla Wafer. There's a little dick in everything. You say the action is on the field, to others it's in the locker room. Sit down, Silly-Dilly.

PRIDE: Well! We name ourselves and others name us! (Pride sits, a little blurred. It fans its nose at Lust. Bob notes with distress that Lust exudes something pungent and moist from a sore, a louse eating its way in. Bob wonders if it will wash out of the upholstery and if so what solvent to use.)

BOB: Don't you think our increasing militarism goes hand in hand with the devaluation of emotion and intimacy?—and rigidity more than any other factor will lead us into nuclear holocaust?

PRIDE-PERSONELLE (plops down on the ground and lies not looking up and cries): Lord, Mercy!

LUST: Honey, you're in the deep freeze waiting for the cure. The only thing left between you and Death is to die.

      The word Death hangs in the air: DEATH. We fall silent, stymied and dejected. The furniture is shaped like cartoon sexual organs. A knock at the door. Lily shoots me a reproachful glance, a message in a bottle that reads, 'I'm trapped.' She huffs and wags but without conviction. We sense an odor of hot oil and oregano. A voice from the Other Side cries out: Pizza! Of course Jack hasn't brought any money even though the pizza was *his* idea. The pizza looks like a kid's drawing of the world. I pay the man. Then, after these thousand hours of nuance and complexity, Jack abruptly fucks me, comes in a minute with the sound of a stifled sneeze and leaves me and my orgasm orbiting, a distant planet, alone and excited. *Loneliness is violence in slow motion.* He says *good-bye* and rolls away.

He has good political credentials we really do play well together I like his books he has beautiful eyes, warm, intelligent, lively, humorous, and when he admits to shared understanding, they twinkle.

Dump him, said Bruce
Dump him, said Denise
Dump him, said Kathy
Dump him, said Sally
Dump him, said Tom

I always felt that I needed only one more clue to convict Jack, one more incident to verify his indifference; incidents came and went, none struck me as definitive.

Bar scene

I ATTENDED SILVANA Nova's '*Chiang Ching*: A Valid Revolutionary Drama.' Silvana is an extravagant man and I guess you could call his interpretation a gay left camp saint's tale, although even modest pressure on the authorized version of Chiang would push her into caricature. Outside the gallery it rained, atypical for September. Rain pelted against the dark skylight and excited us. We were open and expectant.

Silvana starts Chiang out as a Cinderella servant dressed in rags with a burlap babushka. A sad light defines him with its shadow as he holds up some miniature Chinese doll pajamas and cries out to us, 'The little mistress is tired of her outfit and gives it to me. Cast-offs! And for this I am supposed to be grateful—why they don't even fit! Nothing ever fits.

I don't fit!' She wears an expression of utter regret as though to say, 'You mean that's *all* the pleasure for me in life?' So in the next scene she becomes a famous actress—'Oh I thought I was happy, but of course I was only fooling myself'—and then, in a smart cap and enormous glasses, she's an ideologue teaching revolution to factory workers; she underlines with her pointer on the blackboard:

1) stress positive figures
2) of these, stress heroes
3) of these, stress main heroes

Like any drag it was hard to get a level on the illusion and the intention to break illusion, on how much appreciation of Chiang went with how much criticism. Still, Silvana had the wit to present the ambiguity as a puzzle we shared. His play gathered San Francisco's gay left and I felt a continuity with the audience; I was able to recognize myself in them, a tonic for the garish disarray of my recent life. I noticed that when I laughed I traded glances with a man sitting across the room. Abashed, I put myself on hold to watch Chiang go to Yenan, fall in love with Mao and marry him, and compress the Great March into a T'ai Chi ballet; when I turned back he looked right at me and we confirmed our liaison with a smile and a nod.

Meanwhile, Silvana's on the phone: Hello, Madame Witke? No, chou dunno me girl, wait, don't hang up . . . I just read your book about Comrade Chiang Ching. Oh yes, I enjoyed it very much. What?

Oh I think that she was marvelous. Yes, it was a shame . . . You see, I was particularly fascinated by her because of her struggle as a woman, trying to make an inroad into the male-dominated power structure, and her life seems to have been rife with contradiction and then of course . . . yes, the trial!!! Ohmygod, it was better than Judy Holliday before the House UnAmerican Activities Committee. Did she ever work it! There were a few things that somehow got left out of the book. Well, for instance, what kind of shoes did she wear? How were the bathrooms decorated?—

We continued laughing together, a great erotic warmup. He was tall and beaky, with big hands and feet and sandy brown hair. Sometimes his face appeared haggard, other times startlingly resolved. Silvana reclined in light sliced into Deco waves by Venetian blinds, an oceanic glamor; he gave Chiang a throaty Garbo accent: 'Her interpretation of nine-teenth-century bourgeois democratic works is outstanding . . . We have copies of *Camille* and *Queen Christina*, I often view them in conjunction with a documentary I guided in product of recent archeological excavations. In one, the so-called "pickled princess" is unearthed.'

The Cultural Revolution began; when we expected to laugh we looked toward each other in anticipation. I liked the light in his eye, his looseness and willingness. Chiang breaks open a fortune cookie: THERE IS NO SUCH THING AS ART FOR

ART'S SAKE, ART THAT STANDS ABOVE CLASSES, ART THAT IS DETACHED FROM AND INDEPENDENT OF POLITICS. Finally the high drama of the trial. Silvana pulls out all the stops—he's in a gold lamé robe towering in a red spot. One hand points to heaven, 'If you are going to strike a dog, think first of its master. I was Chairman Mao's dog. Whomever he told me to bite, I bit.' His other hand appeals to us as he reprises the MAO LOVE THEME, 'Kiss Kiss Kiss.' He concludes: I have done nothing wrong. I only followed the examples set by the Great Helmsman. I dare you to sentence me to death in front of a million people in Tiananmen Square. Go on, do it! But I have no guilt. I dared to make revolution! And I will succeed!

158

The performance over, Gary and I formally picked each other up; his height surprised me. I liked his gravelly voice, relaxed and quiet as though he were lying down. He told me he was a masseur— good hands!—and we walked to the Stud for a drink.

Our voices were soft; his boots made crisp footsteps, my soft shoes made none. Rain had washed the air—torches and flying flares arrayed the sky and the streets held a clear silence. We opened the Stud's door on, as they say, a different reality. The place was packed; it was hot, smoky and throbbing. We entered the bar but retreated into our separate bodies with an awareness of the space between worlds. After a few drinks we expanded out into the room feeling happy and victorious. I sighted Tom with a big man;

I dare you to sentence me to death in front of a million people in Tiananmen Square. Go on, do it! (p. 158).

Silvana Nova's *Chiang Ching: a Valid Revolutionary Drama*. Photo: John Grau.

Méliès takes his head off and tosses it to the top of the screen where it becomes the globe of an eighth note on a musical staff (p. 175).

Le Mélomane.

both leaned heavily into the bar. Like Tom, his friend was tall, but dark and burly. He pushed Tom and shouted, 'You. Are. One. Nice. Man. Tommy. Tom. You. Are. One. Nice. Man.' To me he seemed threatening. He rubbed his own chest and belly with the familiarity of the totally drunk.

Tom held his palms up in front of the guy's chest thoughtfully, as though warming them at a fire—or could he start one there by sympathetic magic? Then he rose to the occasion and shouted, 'I Am A Sweetheart. A Sweetheart. A Fucking Sweetheart—*Bobby!* I want you to meet someone. Look, isn't he terrific?' Tom's big face suffused with joy— he shouted 'I love you' to the man, then, 'Bobby, we've been seeing each other. For how long?'

His friend raised a misty gaze to the past, 'Since my dog died.'

Tom beamed, 'Isn't he *terrific?*'

Gary and I wanted to dance but at the edge of the dance floor I spotted Jack with (it must be) Joe-Toe. I recognized his blond curls from a photo on Jack's bulletin board. And there I was, trapped in that stupid, plot-ridden turn of events. I writhed backward into the crowd. Joe-Toe did not look happy; Jack was dancing in rapturous oblivion, bopping like a sparrow in a field of bread crumbs, making a small dash this way or that, then a return that became a new feint into a flying hop halfway across the floor. Joe-Toe marked time in the center with the expression of an abandoned Chevy. It seemed odd that Joe-Toe, the object of my meditations, occupied so little physical space. He wore a T-shirt and jeans and Jack wore his good overalls, red chamois shirt and a two-day growth. Jack had warned me that Joe-Toe's visit was going to be very difficult emotionally so he would not be free. I saw myself as the other woman in *As the World Turns*, the one who's a friend of a friend for a few episodes, then on to *Edge of Night* playing the next door neighbor's second cousin. I am an extra and if I don't appear again, no offense.

I started to leave but Jack, in the air, sighted Gary who stood a head taller than the crowd. Gary met Jack's eye, they waved. I only had time to think 'So Gary and Jack—' when Jack caught sight of me and bounded over with an air of music hall *bonhomie* and wrapped me in the exact bear hug I desired when I first met him months before. Joe-Toe and I met. We fiercely averted our eyes or stared too long in each other's worried face; finally we asked a few questions, establishing a rapport that we both knew would see us through this encounter though possibly not longer. I had thought so long about Joe-Toe that I was tired of him. In our battlefield intimacy we shouted over the music, discussing Jack in the third person as he stood there: Jack thinks, Jack says, etc.

I had to piss from nervousness; I navigated through the rising and sinking crowd to the back wall, then into a narrow passage. I tested the air with my nose and followed the dark and deep odor to a toilet with a long urinal trough. The room was dim red, tinted and lit by a single colored bulb level with my eyes; it leered quietly in the noisy darkness. I stood and pissed, carefully ignoring the man next to me. Cold drafts of surprisingly fresh air blew up from somewhere below the urinal in contrast to the sweltering dance floor. The man turned and said hi. Sex? I turned, it was Joe-Toe. He swallowed uneasily. It was strange to see his rosy throat work through so much noise, as though amplification made sound opaque; the red lightbulb and the dryness of his lips retained their silence. There was nothing to do but pretend that we were straight, that Jack did not encumber us, just two guys takin' a piss and shootin' the shit, making friendly dude small talk, facing the same direction on a comradely bus ride. We looked forward, heads up, wearing our vision on the front of our faces while our piss arced down; in the urinal dozens of cigarette filters were pushed here and there by our random tides. The filters were a surprisingly appetizing array of colors. They seemed light for their size—urine sometimes flicked one as though shooting it from a fingernail, or as though it darted away with an angry little life of its own. I restrained an impulse to cross swords. There was no splash, we could have been pissing off a cliff. Two bi-peds pushed out yellow water from tubes. This sudden emphasis on biology was reconciling, like nature.

But Joe-Toe harbored an accusation. His love for Jack was a small territory he had wrested for himself. He studied to recognize what was not loneliness amidst loneliness too gigantic to be readily visible. This region of intimacy was not just a collection of blind spots, so Joe-Toe had to leave its borders more or less undefended. Finally, all buttoned up, he asked, 'Can Jack cry at will?'

I said, 'I don't know, what do you think?'

Joe-Toe rubbed his chin, 'Well, I don't know, all those years at acting school . . .'

Jack wanted to dance and we paired off—Jack and I danced together. He said, 'You know Gary?'

'I don't—we just met.' Jack understood. He stopped and embraced me for a long time on the dance floor, then he held my shoulders to stabilize my head and looked deep into my eyes—it was certainly a deep look but I didn't have a meaning to assign it. Was this forgiveness? *Forgiveness?* I said, 'Jack, I resent you terribly.' He danced away waving gaily; I jumped up lightly to the music and landed hard on his foot. His smile wavered but he saw the joke. They were playing Bonnie Pointer's version of 'Heaven Must Have Sent You': Thank you for the joy you brought me. Two years ago in Los Angeles it had set the tempo to my romance with Brian: Thank you for the things you taught me. My old friendship with that song gave me the leeway to move my body any way inside of it— Heaven must have sent you honey—so I jumped up and landed on Jack's foot again. To love only me. I figured I was entitled to that much. Jack danced over, still smiling. 'Three times won't be funny.' What would three times be? I had never seen him angry or sad or anxious; his emotions had been suitable for general publication. I feel ashamed that I tried to hurt Jack in such a clownish way, and also that I didn't care to persevere. For me, that marked the end of our affair.

He said, 'I try to make my way toward wherever it is I'm not in the company of whomever happens to be absent.'

I SAW JACK again in November. We met at Leon's Soul Food Restaurant to discuss an early draft of this story. Our waiter was white with a thick German accent; he propped himself up on the table with one hand while the other followed my finger to the complete chicken dinner; his face went slack as though he'd never set eyes on the menu before; he read the description to himself, then copied it word for word on his order pad, whispering 'So . . . so . . . so . . .'

Jack wore the good overalls and he was friendly, cuddly, kissy in fact; he beamed at me, winks and nods of shared understanding. Understanding of what? I had a terrible hunch he assumed we were still lovers—certainly his sense of time would allow for that. It was such a tawdry suspicion—how could I know for sure? If I didn't know for sure, how could I tell him we're not? Or maybe he thought he was Joe-Toe's lover? Jack wanted me to change his name. 'But Jack, none of the other characters have different names.'

'For one thing,' Jack replied, 'the finches. You describe the Cordon-Blue Waxbill. *I* never had a Cordon-Blue Waxbill. I never had any birds at all. They belong to my roommate and they are Red-Billed Fire-Finches.'

'Red-Billed Fire-Finches?' I didn't want to pretend I was comfortable with Jack but in the end I was. I felt lighthearted; I knew him so well and at the same time he seemed relegated to a past characterized by suffering, so I could treat him with the careless familiarity of a sibling. Still, I suffered a dart of sweet confusion when our eyes met. He didn't look like death; he looked tender and human.

'From West Africa. Pinkish-red, fading to yellowish brown underneath, with brown wings and tail. The sides are speckled with tiny white dots and of course they have red bills.' Jack's eyes *twinkled*.

'I see what you mean.' I agreed with him; the obstacles to using his real name were insurmountable. I eagerly returned to perceiving Jack as he chose to be perceived, as he revealed himself: *The love story is the tribute the lover must pay the world in order to be reconciled with it.*

'Where did you see Cordon-Blue Waxbills?' Jack asked.

'At the library in a book called *Finches in Color*.'

'Shame,' he said merrily. 'Why all the bird imagery?'

'Jack, I'm a bit embarrassed by that.' My longing for the complete chicken dinner was suddenly qualified. 'The bird symbols reduce you to fiction. The first chapter used to have a love dream that I borrowed from Chaucer. You're an eagle and you tear my heart out and put yours in—but later I deleted it. Then there was Lily the finch hunter, hope springing eternal.' I felt guilty, caught in a lie, as though I failed to convey the truth of Jack, as though someone had a truth like a newel post you reach at the top of a flight of stairs.

He pondered a moment and replied, 'I'd like you to call me Clovis.'

'Clovis.'

'Or Alexander.'

'I think I'll call you Jack.'

'Jack? How weird. That's what everyone called my father.'

'It has the right class background and a flat A. I'd rather use your real name.'

'But I wear a mustache and a beard. The man in this story is clean shaven. I don't see how he has anything to do with me. I don't have a chenille bedspread. I dreamt this morning that we devised a better ending, a happy ending for you and me and Phyllis.'

Devise a happy ending? My high anger returned and raised desire from its death bed. One fire started another: what would a happy ending be? I dropped my hand on the table next to Jack for him to retrieve like a flirtatious handkerchief just as our waiter set down two plates of glistening red thighs, backs, breasts, wings and legs. Three seconds of admiration, then he started to eat. Jack's manners, I observed, were better than mine because unconscious. He could arrive, unaware, two hours late for dinner but he used his knife and fork with grace—I might be above or below that but I was certainly not equal to it. Jack smiled affably. I mentally threw out my arms to him.

'No chenille bedspread?' I cried with wild **167** entreaty. 'You're sure?' What else could I have wrong?

Brian answered that question. After a long wait I received this letter: 'Bob, I have this friend. This friend was mad about a boy in San Francisco. He'd ride the bumper of a Greyhound bus to see him. He thought this was the great passion of his life. My friend lost sleep, he drank, smoked, in & out of depression. Up-Down. You know how it goes. Anyway it was hopeless. The guy made a great point of telling my friend often. So my friend found someone else. And what does his former do? Drive my friend crazy with thoughts of past passion.

'Give me a break Bob. Once you've loved someone as I loved you, you don't stop caring for them. But it will take a while before you and I can think of ourselves as friends. I hope that can happen sometime and that you won't join the ranks of fucked up men doing everything for their own convenience.'

Denise told me she saw Phyllis peering into a dubious cafeteria at the foot of Mission Street. I dreamt: I am flipping through my poetry manuscript just before a reading and I arrive at my high school trigonometry notes. I concentrate on one problem: If this triangle equals your son's life, what equals his death? The solution is narrated by my own voice in its crisp, informational mode and illustrated by visual aids projected on my dream screen: First make the hypotenuse equal to one, and then subtract one from the triangle. As the subtraction progresses, the two remaining sides will close up until they form a straight line which we then take and use as the chalk outline around your son's body.

The dream caught me in its toils—it kept insisting on itself even after I woke up. I can barely say it out loud, my breathing becomes irregular. I worry about how this will affect Phyllis when she reads it.

Joe-Toe gets up naked in his New York apartment and prepares to do his morning sit ups. He drags a heavy oak armchair from the next room, positions it at one end of an oblong rug, lies down on the rug with a pillow under his ass so he won't chafe the tender skin, hooks his feet under the oak rung and begins. His body is sore and unwilling like climbing the hard grade of a hill but after thirty his muscles feel oiled; a light sweat mists him. Around fifty the pain disappears entirely and his mind is released. As usual when his mind is released, he finds himself in the middle of a conversation with Jack. He hasn't seen Jack for months. 'I finally find you home. You haven't called me for weeks. You *say* you want to see me. What about all the *effort* I've made?' Joe-Toe's mental additions and subtractions don't lack for pain, hope, etc., but the essential is that they be exhaustive. Jack replies, his face an allegory of innocence, 'We hardly get a chance to see each other, why spoil it?' Joe-Toe's palms open with helplessness. 'Okay Jack, I'll graph it out: Myself, I'm a circle of doors, all open to go out of or come in. Jack, you are a circle of doors, all closed. Now this is the door where you never invite **169** me over to dinner. This is the one where you treat me worse than your friends. This is when you won't sleep with me. This is when you don't tell me your real age. This is when you stand me up. When you ignore me when I'm sick. When you leave town without saying good-bye. This is when you spend my money. This is when you say you want a black lover. This door is when you unplugged the phone. This is when you won't have a personal conversation . . .'

What goes around comes around: Méliès
replicates his image, spins on his heel and
vanishes

170 OH LOVE IS a traveler, a traveler on a
river, a river of no return. Of course there's a lot to be
said *about* a love story because the stakes are so clear:
hold the story up, view it from one angle—happiness.
From another—misfortune. Then banality sets in: I
loved one who loved me not. Or emotional opportunism, the upward mobility of interior life with its cargo
of uniqueness and isolation. Or beneath love's high
scrutiny the selves (one's materials) fly apart; or habit
is stripped away revealing selves that were always
multiple in response to the world's mixed message.
To merely record what happened requires an imagi-
native effort similar to being in love. But what's the
point of a love story?—that I can't be a lover until my
story is known? That it throws light on yours?—or
better, that it rhymes with yours, a story like yours,

something that happened to a friend, an acquaint-ance?—you heard it abbreviated from 'I Only Have Eyes For You' to 'Cry Me a River'? Does it represent you—like a lawyer? Is a story appealing because like a mirror it includes its own forgetting, turning the pain and pleasure into fable?

Society wants its stories; I want to return to society the story it has made—if unhappy, as a revenge, a critique. When orgasms appear to be *produced* by society there are stories about orgasms; ditto identity. Joe-Toe wound up on his hands and knees giving me a blow job. Maybe he thought he was sucking the cock of the void. He called me after Jack gave him a story by Bruce called 'My Walk With Bob.' What intrigued him, he said, was a scene depicting my rapport with the void in which I'm standing at the counter of the Noe Valley Market weighing cucumber prices against textures against looks in the shipment of the day. Inviting Joe-Toe to spend the night was a mere formality; we were both attracted. **171**

It was competent gay sex; a little of this, a little of that, oh oh oh—spurt spurt spurt, then we both lay back for our moment of composure. I admired his ripply belly as I admire courage or intelligence but our pacing was out of sync and we knew the encounter had exhausted the permutations. Joe-Toe liked drama, flailing right from the first kiss—he dashed from position to position adhering to an agenda I never really grasped, and I wondered how it meshed with Jack's well-wishing, avuncular sexuality.

Although Joe-Toe and I had spent our erotic allotment we still had plenty of friendliness left. I turned off the light. Jack had been the subject of our previous conversation and we returned to him but this time with tangled legs and my hand draped over Joe-Toe's stomach in post-coital intimacy. In fact, I was more attracted to his cool belly and blondness now that the possibility of sex lay behind us and we were falling asleep together so sweetly. I confessed that I was privy to his nickname. Joe-Toe wondered if Jack had given me a new name. Well, yes, Jack had renamed both of his lovers. Joe-Toe asked me what that name was. I replied reluctantly 'Macho Peaches.'

'   '

'After the poem by Neruda and an image from my "Sex Story."'

'What image?'

I found myself rubbing my chin like Jack, like Joe-Toe. 'Uh, someone compares my ass to a peach.'

He laughed. We both laughed: Macho Peaches and Joe-Toe laughed. Ringlets spilled on my shoulder. I suddenly saw Jack's point of view, how it might be desirable to have the warmth and magazine curls in my bed night after night. 'In return for our names I think we should have given Jack a disease.'

'Yes,' Joe-Toe said, 'like Martin did.'

'What?' I turned on the light.

Joe-Toe's face slowed down and stopped. *'Martin?'*

He sat up—he protested—he reddened—he was sworn to secrecy—he couldn't possibly—Jack would never—finally he relented but he made me promise (the classic exchange) never to breathe a word. 'I promise,' I said, a straightforward lie. I'd had sex with Martin a few times and could have pieced together Jack's experience but I gave first place in my imagination to Bruce's expression, the attention he would give to every turn of this new and *shocking* development, the questions to polish each facet of revelation, to draw morals, to stretch the moment like taffy—'Now did you say Joe-Toe earns his living as a *stage* actor?' Bruce asks carefully. I would get excited: I was stunned, Bruce, stunned—you know what he said then? (Bruce draws back to prolong the disclosure.) That Jack had three long term lovers, Jack *lied* to me, and not only that . . .(Here Bruce assumes an expression of not quite sincere shock.) Jack had orgies and fuck-buddies—Suddenly Bruce and I break into laughter as though I'd capped a long private joke. The laughter is really about intimacy and the pleasure of friendship.

Joe-Toe rubbed his chin and said, 'Martin's the art critic, right?'

'Yes.'

'That's him then. Did Jack meet him at some party?'

'At Bruce's.'

'They made a date—and they went out—'

'*And?*'

'And later Martin sent Jack a letter. Martin said that he had a problem.'

'Did that problem have a name?'

'Gonorrhea and that Jack was infected and he asked Jack not to tell you about their dates.'

'They had more than one?'

My feelings backflipped almost palpably. I viewed Cyrus as a reason to mistrust Jack, Martin as a reason to love him. Now these relationships were altered, reinterpreted. Martin, with his fancy talk about Greuze and Chardin! I was wronged—a caricature of betrayal. I tried 'How could you!' on for size. I prodded my emotions but I couldn't find a sore place. Oh well, *no news is good news*. But Jack's infamy delighted me from the standpoint of sheer plot. Now that he'd made a fool of me, our story was complete. I plied Joe-Toe with questions; he opened the closet of Jack's love life and facts and orgasms tumbled out into the room. They were like new vocabulary. I tried different combinations. Jack had outright lied. That relieved me since it helped to shape the nebulous unhappiness I had felt. Yet his dishonesty still seemed intangible. Did he believe himself? Was his so-called fear of disease actually a reluctance to infect me? To reinfect himself? But he'd been afraid before the party—or had he? Still, his interest in sex made some sense of my attraction to him. Events once again seemed fluid and reversible; I was excited; suddenly I could reach, hold, contain, drop and know. My rising spirits alarmed Joe-Toe. I said gravely, 'They were punished in those parts wherein they sinned.' I wonder what Jack will think when he reads this—or Martin for that matter. *The more violently Cupid has pierced and branded me, the better I shall avenge the wound he has made.*

Once Jack and I attended an evening of early silents. In one a magician struts onto a stage. The image of the magician and the stage wavers and adjusts and wavers as though contending against that primary light of silent movies, but the magician is secure, exhibitionistic, preening, self-confident. The world with its veils of illusion is in danger, not him. Although the auditorium was filled with piano music and a roar of scuffing, coughs and whispers, around the magician it's so silent that even breath is intrusive. **175** Besides being the only actor, he's also the director of the movie; his name is Méliès although I would call him Desire. The film medium offers no resistance to the flexibility of his imagination but his images are merely contemplative, his continuity false because it doesn't measure and overcome the world's real gravity and resistance to change. Méliès takes his head off and tosses it to the top of the screen where it becomes the globe of an eighth note on a musical staff. Another head appears on his neck; he removes it and tosses it up and so on. Each identical head conducts its own gabby conversation, each with its goals and urgency and point of view; perhaps one talks about biology's delicate chemical braiding and another about left politics and another about commodity life and another about loneliness—get the idea? They are all yacking, self-absorbed, small beards accentuating the working of their mouths. They seem affronted and reproachful but their grievance takes a collective form charting out a crude melody—call it 'Meaning'—with heads as notes and the song increasingly legible rather than audible, *at once a made up thing and a depth in which my being is.* Jack took my hand. In flickering darkness I laid his hand on my thigh. I considered his apt profile with fond possession and he replied with a dilated twinkle that caught light from the screen. In front of us a woman absentmindedly stroked her lover's collar; down the aisle a man draped his arm around his neighbor's shoulders; all around me people touched sleeves, shoes, nonchalantly called each other honey or sweetheart with all that implies, a piece of skin admired, licked, nibbled, getting hungry together, shared orgasms, shared telephone bills, querulous voices. Then the process reverses itself. Méliès summons each head back to his shoulders where it disappears to make room for the next and the next; inspiration fails along with the will to sustain a contradiction—head by head, no melody, no magician.

Mine is an art of collage; I invite you to register changes of tone and century. For acknowledgements, numerous as stars and stranger bedfellows, here's an incomplete list of writers and works present one way or another: George Bataille's *Death and Sensuality;* Robert Venturi's *Learning from Las Vegas;* Denis Diderot's art criticism and the theories about it in Michael Fried's *Absorption and Theatricality;* small reworkings from Charles Baudelaire's "At One O'Clock in the Morning," Lafcadio Hearn's *Kwaidan*, the letters of Neil Voegtle; snippets from Ovid's *Art of Love*, John F. Karr's "Porn Corner" in the "Bay Area Reporter," more gleanings from "Drummer" and "Numbers," Goethe's *Elective Affinities* and Roland Barthes' *A Lover's Discourse*.

Chapters from *Jack the Modernist* have appeared in *Advocate Men*, *Five Fingers Review*, *No Apologies*, *Zyzzyva*, and *Ottotole*.

R.G.